THE HARDER THE PAIN

Une compilation

Broken Happy and The Unraveling

The Loftier the Goal, the Harder the Pain

CONTENTS

OBSESSION

The phone rang a second time in less than a minute. The insistent ringing shattered José's light reverie and woke him up for good this time. He was not going to sleep late that day. In any case, the sun was already beaming, warming the still Dominican Republic air. He'd gone to his homeland, four hours away from Virginia by plane, for two weeks to visit his elderly mother.

"Hello."

"Good morning José. How are you?"

It was one of the kids, and she breathed heavily into the phone. It was nine; Esma had no qualms about calling early. She must have thought, he was awake. Anyway, staying in bed past 7 am wasn't like him.

"I'm well, thank you. You? Why are you calling?"

"We've missed you. You're coming back in

two days, right?"

José frowned and scratched his head. What were his step-children up to? "Yeah, that's right. What can I do for you, Esma?"

"There's a house I showed Mom online. I want you to see it too and promise that the day after you return we can all go and see it. There is an open house. Promise?"

"Okay, we shall. What's really going on?"

14-year-old Esma and, her little sister, 10-year-old Ayse, were José's wife's children from a previous marriage. Bright girls, that behaved like princesses, and preferred to be called BRATs—Beautiful Rich American Turks. Bratty as they were, more than anyone realized, he considered them his girls too. José adored them.

"Nothing. I really can't wait for you to see it. That's all. See you in two days then. Bye, José."

"Bye, beautiful."

There was nothing José would not do for her. Precious as she was, Esma had no business disturbing him like this. Yet, they had an affinity for each other.

José rolled his shoulders and climbed out of bed. He thought it strange. She'd never interrupted his vacation before. And for what?

A trivial promise! Why did his wife, Emel, allow the international call? Something was up! Sure, they would all go and see some random house?

He shook his head. Whatever was up, he knew his wife was more than likely behind it. José pressed his palms into his eyes and then ran his fingers through his hair. He had wanted to get away from it all. Unhappy at work, disgusted with his professional situation because of a superior he found toxic, he'd come up with the perfect excuse to get away. He needed time off to take care of his aging mother. The thought of her, past age seventy, living alone far from close relatives, without the benefit of good health, was a major source of irritation.

José worried about Esmeralda, his valiant mother. Ensanche Naco, in the capital, Santo Domingo, his hometown, was a very upscale and cosmopolitan neighborhood. Over the last decade it had undergone a radical transformation. High-rise residential and office buildings had sprouted at a rate so alarming the sudden elevation in population density caused unprecedented traffic congestion. José had barely recognized the place.

Before the 1990s, the upper-middle-class neighborhood had consisted of low-rise buildings and large family homes. Esmeralda's house was now too big for one person. José remembered, in better days, seven people had lived there: her husband, herself, their three children and a gardener/handyman, and finally his wife, the maid, who also cooked for the family. But now Esmeralda could no longer take care of it, or pay someone to do it.

It remained a large house, but had lost its purpose. The mansion no longer felt like a home. It even sounded different: mostly quiet, except for the crackling noises the wood made and the murmur of the wind against the windows. Three of the six bedrooms in the back remained locked at all times, out of sight and out of mind, creating all kinds of concerns over potential break-ins. Some stranger could be sleeping in the mansion and his mother would be none the wiser.

José knew that a considerable number of city residents lived in abject poverty, much too close for comfort, in neighborhoods a stone throw away. Neglected by her progeny long before her husband's passing, in a country that lacked a national retirement and a healthcare system, for immediate assistance Esmeralda relied on a host of distant relatives and younger cousins. José knew that, for the most part, all of them hoped for a piece of her inheritance.

José's older sister had long ago moved with her husband to New York City. The younger one had settled in Chicago, and he'd made roots in Virginia. Esmeralda remained in good spirit, yet he could not forgive himself; he felt guilty for leaving her behind. He'd moved too far up north in search of opportunity; exactly what she had encouraged them to do when he was a teenager.

At her insistence they, José and his sisters, had agreed not to return and settle to an island that could not support their big dreams. He now regretted agreeing to this. The island looked vibrant. Economic growth had returned bringing riches to more professionals, not just to a handful of musicians and celebrity baseball players. The warmth outside did not compare to the oppressive July heat in Virginia.

José felt home here. No, he was home.

The morning of Esma's call, he went to the beach and swam a few laps, a welcome break from a busy week sorting, with a practiced eye, his mother's affairs. He had spent the last week poring over taxes, bank notices and contractual agreements. He helped her with the bureaucratic hassle much like his father had done before him for fifty years. The ownership of sugar cane plantations in the western part of the country inherited from her father generated much red tape. Rumor had it, scores of Haitian obradoras routinely lost their lives there, eaten whole by the discriminating fields.

After the swimming, he walked over to his favorite eat-out joint on the beach and gulped a delicious lunch of spicy pescado frito, red snapper with red beans and rice, and a side of plantain. Satisfied, craving no more, he brought a plate home for Esmeralda. He loved his native food. It sang in his mouth, and filled him in a way American food never could. His soul craved it. Nothing in Virginia could rival with home. A native land feels sacred. In his mind Virginia stood for order and the rule of law, while the DR, for passion and sensuality. These two hardly ever mixed.

He missed it all, especially the food; the fish, the tasty asopao, the seasoned meat, and the shellfish. He binged on Batata fritas, liqueur, Mamajuana, and freshly pressed tropical juices. In two short weeks, José would put on a few pounds of happy.

Finally, all was in order. The day before he flew back to America, he consented to do one last thing for his mother. She was a good Catholic. A tradition she insisted on keeping whenever her son came for a visit; he would accompany her to the "dump". It was a way, as good as any, for them to stay grounded, and to give thanks and praise to a merciful God who had blessed and kept the family safe through uncertain times.

Many families had not been as lucky as José's family. For many, the Dominican Republic was a tropical piece of hell. Illiterate bottom feeders, many people only a notch above "gusanos," worms, faced extreme hardship. They made their living off of the large landfill where the city trash disappeared. José remembered people digging through piles upon piles of discarded items in search of anything worth recycling and selling.

Despite the stench, they hardly ever left the dump for fear someone would rob them of the bounty. Businesses came to them and paid for the most useful and salvageable finds. So did sinners looking for absolution, eager to assuage their conscience by delivering food and water to people in greater need. The night before, Esmeralda and José with the help of a few cousins loaded batches of bottled water and canned goods onto Toyota pickup trucks and brought them to the 'dump'.

"All will be better now," said Esmeralda.

Humbled, later that night, José had the best sleep he'd had in a while. The next morning, a flight took him back to the life he had made in Virginia. The trip back home lasted less than five hours. By two in the afternoon, he'd already stashed away his suitcase in a closet. In two days he would be returning to the office. His relationship with the deputy turned sour and trouble started once management found out about his office romance with Emel. José felt crushed and collapsed on the bed trying not to think about it.

José had met Emel at work, in the deputy chief's office. If one paid close attention, this much was obvious, Emel herself could barely stand the surly man or the office. She wore her emotions on her sleeves. With such an expressive face, José surmised, she was not much of a politician. Like most staff, she found it hard to maintain a poker face. Always of a mind to punish someone, Waldo never uttered a word of appreciation, nor did he trust his charges to do what is right. He looked for flaws in everything anyone did or said.

Uneasy around the old man, Emel felt that he very much wanted to get her in trouble at the first opportunity, and keep her confined to a life of dissatisfaction at work. Over the littlest thing, Waldo was constantly on her case, as if he intended to make her life miserable and have her quit. She was new to the job and had no history with the company. "What was the real issue? Was he trying to show her who's boss?

Something was the matter with this man!"
Emel was everything anyone would want for
an employee; competent, bright, pleasant and
attractive. "That's it! Maybe Waldo secretly
fancied her? She must've stopped or
discouraged his not so subtle advances."

When José first showed up in the office of
the new chief of the IT Training Branch, an
athletic and charismatic fellow, it was to
negotiate the hand-off of a series of courses in
need of a new host. The chief was energetic,
alert, and young. In a corner of the large office,
witnessing the pitch sat Waldo, the deputy
chief, a sullen character withdrawn into an
uncomfortable chair attempting to suppress a
snarl.

Five minutes into the pitch — a hastily
prepared presentation of the benefits students
derived from the courses José had designed and
delivered — the chief interrupted to extend a
generous job offer on the spot. It befuddled
José. He had not sought a position, merely a
new host for the courses he was giving away.
Without one, his efforts would have gone to
waste. He promised, however, to consider the
job offer.

The first time he met him, José could see
that Waldo's demeanor betrayed an inner

tension. He'd remained withdrawn, aloof, almost timid. He sensed an uneasiness whenever he approached the man. Was it personal? Waldo's closed off attitude affected everyone around him. Did he resent him too? Barely perceptible hints betrayed how much he resented his younger superior, the chief of the IT Training Branch. Why the attitude?

Waldo had coveted the position someone in headquarters had led him to believe would naturally fall into his lap, only to see it go to a bolder candidate half his age. He'd suffered what he saw as a humiliation! By keeping silent, save for a few twitches, while everyone in his vicinity sensed it, he faked it and managed to mostly hide his growing frustration. He would remain the deputy for the time being. To survive the office, he sported a good-natured grandfatherly persona, yet succeeded in fooling only a few people. His frustration turned into a subdued rage which in the course of eight months prompted him to come up with no fewer than a couple of dozen excuses to justify repeated absences.

The two secretaries who fielded his calls grew a nose for Waldo's next absence and excuse, which became legendary.

"We've been competing to see who collects the lamest excuse from the deputy." Said the oldest. To which the youngest responded:

"I'm pretty sure I'm winning. On two occasions, he used the excuse "I hurt my back yesterday trying to get my 7" wooden fence gate back onto its hinges. I won't be able to get into my little car this morning" forgetting he'd already used it once before. How could this not be the lamest?"

Eager for a clear winner they engaged everyone in the gossiping.

"Not so fast. You be the judge, José. How about these? "I will not be in today. After the devastating news that I was not selected as chief, I need a day at home." And this one, "I cannot warm up this morning. I will be home." And that one, "I hurt my back in the cold working on a car yesterday. I will be home with email access."

"That one is funnier, I think, "Well, whatever was bothering me since lunch yesterday has caught up with me. I will be out today."

And they bickered on and on. Colleagues joined in the fun.

"God forbid anyone in the office has an emergency or a legitimate reason to miss work, like I did when my wife went into labor last month. Waldo hounded me on the phone, and treated me like a delinquent. He even threatened to write me up. This man would've sent the national guards after me if he could have." The office had a good laugh at Waldo's expense.

José wanted to get away from that place for good, but felt trapped. To disagree with the deputy was tantamount to risking a promotion. Worse, he held grudges. The absence of flattery, a lack of deference, bothered him to no end. Insecure to the core, Waldo had to be the center of all the attention. The deputy was utterly toxic. An angry shrinking man, a negative figure, José resented his actions even more after finding out that indeed, he'd tried to destroy his chances of ever getting promoted.

During the past couple of months preceding his visit to the DR, José had found it particularly difficult to work with Waldo. In that, he was hardly alone. He had allies; all the people whose careers he tried to stunt. Mainly, the blatant disregard shown to the people under him accounted for the man's unpopularity. The grandfatherly stance deceived no-one. His higher ups after a while stopped trusting him too. José resented Waldo the most for assuming that he hated him. Did he believe himself important enough to occupy precious real estate in José's head, and mobilize this much animus? Hatred was a big deal. It required effort and a commitment. Hate? That emotion was exhausting. One had to care enough. The assumption alone caused José to become thoroughly disgusted with Waldo's obsession with himself.

Early on, as if looking for an ally, throughout the day, Emel would hover and seek out José's advice; until one day, she mustered the courage to ask him out. It was a risky thing to do, asking someone out at the office. José could have been a lout, who crushed her pride, and disgraced her publicly. In an office this small and so conservative, a public rejection would have destroyed her reputation and made her pass for the workplace slut. But José agreed to the date.

Emel loved to cook. She'd invited him over for dinner. First, she'd get him hooked on her cooking, then, she'd play it by ear. Pouring wine over a delicious middle eastern meal José had been praying for time to slow down to a halt. He was enjoying himself. Who knew Emel could be so much fun? How could one resist these sultry eyes? Deny the Lust? The temperature had been rising. José struggled to remain phlegmatic, appear detached, and feign a lack of real interest. Her looks held the promise of a boundless rapture. She reeled him in, and seemed skilled in all the areas that made a woman luring to a man. The initial spark between them ignited a compelling chemical brushfire which unfurled into a full-fledged carnal firestorm. That evening long before they were wed, José and Emel caught a case of the fever.

Emel embodied exuberance. A colorful full-figured character, she was large and in charge. He loved the way she made him feel. With her shimmying, playful and oversized buttock, she kept him riveted and at attention. Her scent became enough to excite him. He felt increasingly lost without her. Of average height, 5'5, the butterscotch complexioned, curvaceous Turkish American woman may have looked fat to some, but to José, she was divinely scrumptious; happy in her own skin, and it showed. Her towering personality mesmerized him. Built for lovemaking, Emel had an Ashley Graham quality to her looks, a cute face, and fully kissable lips. José considered her supremely sexy. She reigned over his libido and nighttime fantasies. The boy was happy to have been whipped.

From Istanbul, Turkey, and proud of it, Emel often passed for a Latina in the U.S. The first time José saw her, he mistook her for a Latina, much like others before him had done, and greeted her in Spanish. Pictures of Atatürk and the evil eye hung in every room of her townhouse. The dark blue teardrop-shaped piece of glass, with an intense black pupil over white appeared on clothing, furniture, and jewelry. The talisman provided peace of mind and warded off bad spirits. A beauty queen with status, Emel was a part of the Turkish elite, but had given up a career as a diplomat for a poor ambitious immigrant, Kadir, she'd met at an embassy function in Washington. She'd believed in the man's vision.

With the connections she'd made over the years, and after the wedding, she helped Kadir grow a solid import/export business that made him a millionaire within ten years. Before the kids arrived, Emel and Kadir had grown to enjoy the good life together; they took trips abroad whenever they felt like it, slept in fancy hotels, drank champagne, ate caviar, drove exotic cars, developed expensive tastes, and fulfilled their wildest fantasies. Nothing was too good for either of them. Proud Ottomans, a people with a rich history of conquests and a strong sense of identity, they saw themselves as deserving of the best.

Once the children came, Emel's jet-setting screeched abruptly to a halt, while Kadir's continued. Her only concern, Keeping the nest warm. More often than Emel cared for Kadir's business trips landed him halfway around the world, far from home and family. She wanted him home, she claimed, for the sake of the children. They were growing so fast.

Celebrating a deal made with business partners at a club in Slovenia, one day, Kadir bumped into a gorgeous blonde. Spellbound, in the sudden mood for play, he removed his ring and then cast a strong line. Flashing potent aphrodisiacs, money, power, and status, that instant, the die was cast. His marriage to Emel was doomed.

Emel eventually found out about the love nest and the woman he hid in plain sight, tipped off by Kadir's renewed attention to his appearance. He'd moved his mistress stateside. Bleeding pride, she taught herself a few unfortunate lessons: Louis Vuitton bags over flowers, and flowers over cards; stick around with a man only as long as times were good and never when times were bad. Feeling short-changed, now more than ever, she aspired to an exclusive lifestyle. A man in need of emotional support would have to call his mama, not her.

Emel was no man's comforter. She only had daughters.

Under these circumstances, remarriage was not to bring her happiness. José learned that the hard way. Emel never chose happiness, a cheap emotion, as a single woman or as a married woman. She didn't know how. True happiness to her, it seemed, had always been more about owning things. There was so much stuff yet to be had. Marriage never worked for unhappy greedy people expecting their partners to make them whole. Only happy people made happy marriages. A fury in bed, Emel's bliss partly required José to climb on top of her, alert and responsive to her every need. She surrendered then, stopped talking and let go of inhibitions.

While José yearned for the crisp clean air of his native land the Dominican Republic, and craved the foods, the smells, and the golden warmth that would seep into your bones, Emel's happiness relied on things bought: diamonds, clothes and purses..

José knew that Emel would never love his homeland. It was too poor. Most times, she romanticized the past, before "the blonde bitch" came around and shattered a picture-perfect-family. The memory of that past crept up and forced her ex-husband upon José as the hero in a life she hung onto. She wallowed in self-pity causing José to bear the cost of another man's transgressions. She talked as if she'd been skinned alive and had yet to recover. Over time, her heavy heart built up an invisible wall of unmet expectations too tall and too exhausting to climb over.

Esma and Ayse would not stop talking about the house and how perfect it looked. To bolster her big sister's claim, on her MacBook Ayse pulled up pictures of a mansion. The oversized five-bedroom house was 5,577 square feet and sat on a four-acre lot somewhere in Hamilton, Virginia, a tiny rural town in western Loudoun County 50 miles west of Washington, DC. A mile-long quaint narrow town, inhabited by no more than 600 people a couple of miles from the Potomac River.

José had grown up in a mansion and wasn't much impressed with them. They had a way of grounding you to a place, making it difficult to pick up and go. His heart was already in the DR. There was no way he'd entertain an idea that could only deepen his roots in the U.S. It was way too early to share these private feelings with Emel. Sharing feelings could backfire. Home is where the heart is; his was with

Esmeralda, his mother. To get some peace, José kept the promise he'd made to Esma and drove the girls to the mansion.

Upon arriving at the house, Emel's smile broadened. Although the children seemed to be leading the way, José knew that his wife had a heavy hand in the sudden collective infatuation. The house looked impressive, even more appealing than it did online. Its open floor, sunroom, many windows, and sunroofs brought a lot of light inside. Throughout the house the details were thrilling: granite, recessed lighting, spacious rooms, pricey upgrades, mahogany floors, intricate finishes, high ceilings, a humongous finished basement, breakfast bar, loft, study, a fully renovated kitchen complete with an oversized island, expansive deck, comfy media room, in-ground swimming pool, hot tub, and a wet bar. All of the details made José dizzy. He paused, beyond impressed.

The kids running from room to room were beaming. Emel's eyes glistened, wet with giddiness; barely containing her excitement, almost drooling, José knew she'd pictured herself living there many times before. Overwhelmed with adrenaline rushing through his brain, he felt set up.

"Do you like it?" Ayse asked as she tugged

on his shirt.

"Yes. I like it. Very much!"

Back in Ashburn at the townhome, as if to cuddle, Emel inched closer on the couch.

"Honey, we can afford this house." She only called him honey when she wanted something. His BS meter went up. "Between the two of us, we can afford the required $3,000 a month. You sell your condo, I sell this townhouse, and it's done, we won't be paying much more individually than what we're already paying. It is so much bigger, so much more beautiful. You deserve this. Let's buy it. Honey please."

She trailed a finger across his chest. He smiled at her, knowing there was no point in arguing. "I think you're right. When you put it like that, it seems doable. The price tag is scary though, $839,900. Let me think about it."

José was buying time. True, they could all use more space. The 2,500-square-foot townhouse was adequate for two adults and two kids, but all the stuff Emel and the kids had accumulated over the years was making it feel cramped. There was stuff everywhere and no plan to donate or do away with any of it. Almost three years in that townhouse and José still did not feel at home, but rather uncomfortable. Expensive gadgets everywhere cluttered his thoughts, making him long for the simplicity of his mother's house.

His belongings were in storage, it made sense to upgrade. José's thoughts drifted back to the dump and the people who would wade through the trash hoping to find enough to make a living. The thought of more debt triggered visions of indentured servitude like the kind he'd seen on his family's sugar cane plantations. Uncertainty triggered anxiety; not so much the monthly payments, but the future scared him, adding to the sense that his relationship with Emel was tittering on the brink of failure.

She seemed oblivious, unconcerned with any of that. Maybe she was. He couldn't afford to throw caution to the wind and let his guard down; feeling like he was in another man's shoes, a richer man, playing father to his progeny and frolicking with his wife. She still raged at the 'real' husband's infidelity.

Emel hated the blonde, her ex's new wife and mother of his newborn baby boy. A boy she couldn't give him. The Slovenian bitch as she called her, the one he'd dared bring under her nose across the Atlantic Ocean, to reinvent himself, feel young again, and inhabit their dream. No one in the townhouse was to speak her name.

Anja, Anja.

A mere allusion to Anja's existence would throw the household into hell-bending turmoil. Although remarried, emotionally Emel was stuck. She had not moved on and couldn't let go of the past. José was just a tool. The hatred she nurtured for her ex and his new woman stunted the growth of the commitment she'd made to him three years in. José saw this new house business as just another test he was sure to flunk.

It required a bet on a future he felt ill-equipped to take on. Now, with the shenanigans going on at home, he gave no thought to work unless he had to. What if he lost his job? What if their divergent aspirations could not be reconciled? They disagreed on everything, priorities included. He was stifling. They shared no children of their own, no vision of a clear future. Nothing more than great affection and an inextinguishable lust. She wanted to retire in Turkey; he wanted to go back to Esmeralda. Would he need to give up on the marriage to be happy?

José would continue to buy time and find out why, all of a sudden, this new house had become a wedge between them, a huge deal that added to the turmoil in their lives. Seeing his excitement waning, Esma insisted they are again going to see the beautiful house the following weekend.

So they did.

And this time, as he slowly and quietly paced each room, José tried as hard as he could to imagine himself living there with Emel and the kids.

He would try harder to hang on to the hope of a good relationship. It was the hardest thing to do. That mansion was designed for a rich happy family. His marriage felt like a fraud based on lust; try as he might, he could not see himself in it over the long haul. It was a question of values. In the car, on the way back to Ashburn, escaping the hard questions would prove impossible.

Emel turned to him all glammed up for the occasion. "Honey, I can't wait for us to live in this house. We're gonna be so happy there."

The girls piped in to press for a response. Lost in his thoughts, José tried out loud to add up the higher property tax with the cost of keeping the house cool in the summer and warm in the winter; he would not be disturbed. He still had to put a son through college, and before indulging any further felt the need to get to the bottom of his wife and kids' obsession.

"Esma, why now, all of a sudden? What's different now?"

From the back of the six-year-old Benz S 500:

"Why are you not on board, José? This is the American dream. Stop acting like an immigrant. You are an American now. Own it." Emel rolled her eyes in disbelief, repressing her annoyance.

Ayse erupted. "I knew it, mom. Your husband thinks small. He's a little man."

"Why does it matter so mooch to you guys that we get this particular house?" José said.

Under pressure and exasperated, his Spanish accent resurfaced.

"Well," Esma said, "if you must know, my father moved into a much bigger house with his new family recently. And we agreed, my sister, my mom and I, that we too deserve to live in a bigger house."

"Aye, caramba! I see."

In frustration Emel blurted out, "Stop being so cheap, José. We can afford this new house. What is wrong with you?"

The next day, in the early afternoon, José instructed everyone to get in his car. It was Sunday and to brighten the heavy and somber mood, they would be heading to a water park a few miles away to enjoy an afternoon outside. The sun and some fresh air, he told them, would do wonders for this family!

He felt adventurous, promised them a good time, and asked everyone to chill out and for once appreciate the simple things in life. As a kid growing up in the Dominican Republic, he'd seen his share of poverty all around, especially in the bateys* his mother owns. He developed an appreciation for the good fortune that had befallen his family. He knew things could be much worse.

They had to hurry if they were to avoid crowds and arrive early. During weekends in the summertime, water parks tended to be crowded. Chlorine and pH readings being what they were, José cautioned the kids to be careful not to swallow park water.

"Our day at the park is not limited to the water and the sun! Enjoy the playground. I'm sure you'll find plenty to do there!" José laughed, and then turned to his wife. "You'll find high back sand chairs, and chaises-longues spread throughout the park. And when you need to get out of the sun, there are plenty of shaded areas. Let's meet back at the car when you're done. Two hours from now, everyone."

They could already hear the sound of water

---

* Settlements around a sugar mill

splashing everywhere. The car was even moving slowly under a cascade. Everybody seemed miffed, except José. He was smiling broadly.

"What is this?" Emel asked in disbelief. They were at the carwash.

UNDERAGE

"Why did she get kicked out? She gets A's."

"No, she doesn't. She's not as good as you think, Michael. Clearly."

"You are a liar. What are you talking about, chump? I took classes with that girl. She' a real nerd. Always first in everything."

"Oh, yeah? My bad, you're right. She was the first to get caught, her panties down to her ankles, getting banged by a grown cat in the girls' bathroom."

"That can't be!"

On the phone, the assistant principal had asked her mother to come pick her up from her office where she'd been all morning. When she showed up, Jessica refused to get into the car. "And I thought you'd understood," yelled her mom. "Girl, don't you walk away from me." Jessica walked home every day. Nothing would be different this day, except this time she would walk the few miles alone.

Other pupils, girls from the same neighborhood, also walked in small groups the few miles that took them home, chatting and carrying on as usual about the rumors at school. That day, Jessica was all everyone wanted to talk about.

"Yo, dis girl's a skank. Do anyone know the name of the man caught with her?"

"No one saw his face. He was wearing some type of face mask and took off too quickly. People say he' a mechanic. He had on a uniform. I guess the police be looking for his sorry ass."

"That girl be in a lot of trouble, for sure."

Jessica walked home alone.

She rehashed the many warnings she'd received about staying away from boys. Yet she had fallen prey to sweet words of flattery and the insistent lust of a charming adult suitor. At home that evening, bracing for the worst, Jessica resigned herself to face the music, and the entire family assembled for the inauspicious occasion, to discuss her fate. She knew she was a disappointment, and kept her gaze down. She could smell the disappointment on them, and she wondered if they could smell the shame on her. No doubt, she reeked of it.

Auntie Brenda, a secretary at one of the local churches, her least favorite relative, spoke first suggesting she be sent out of state to a boarding school. Jessica's aunt had lost her only child, a toddler, in a moment of thoughtless inattention; and now Jessica suspected she resented her sister for holding on to her own. It would have been easier to feel sorry for another's loss than for her own.

The June heat had been suffocating that day, while her Auntie reeling from the warmth, felt a sudden compulsion to take a cold shower. So she had undressed and stepped into the half-empty tub, picked up her child and turned the faucet on. Minutes later, panicked, unable to hold on because of the effect of water on the soap, Auntie Brenda watched powerlessly, in slow motion agony, her slippery baby wriggle loose out of her grip and tumble to the bottom as his little head hit the tub with a thud. Jessica knew the incident had changed her aunt's personality, making her disagreeable in the extreme.

Pete, Jessica's uncle, the family disciplinarian, said reform school would be more appropriate. Her mother who'd been sobbing the whole time indicated she wanted to stop sending her to school altogether. Obviously, she wasn't thinking straight, but no one said anything. Her heart could not bear further humiliation. The family resumed discussing Jessica as if she were not there; as if she were a thing to be tossed about and dismissed. No one agreed on anything. Jessica was only sixteen. With precociously heavy breasts, she could pass for a grown woman.

"She is much too young and immature to stop school. How can she be expected to fend for herself without an education? No, no, there has to be another way!" Her youngest and favorite aunt, Mina, finally said.

Jessica was thankful someone was finally on her side. She continued to stare at her feet and the ugly green carpet in her parent's living room. She hated the world at that instant. Unfocused, yearning to be in her lover's arms, she would've given anything to fly away and escape this torture.

Jessica's father who had not said a word, sullen, sitting alone away from the rest of the group, no longer a real part of the family, having moved out moons ago, had been invited more as a courtesy. No one was truly interested in anything he had to say. He was late with child support and kept staring at the girl who he was now of a mind to disown, looking for an excuse not to have to pay altogether; wondering what he had done to God to heap and deserve such dishonor. Pete, the maternal uncle, opened his mouth again and proclaimed that his niece's behavior called for the severest of reprimands.

"Now this, and then what?"

Spare the rod, spoil the child type thing. As could be expected, he volunteered to chastise the wayward child. Corporal punishment used effectively does not have to amount to child abuse, he insisted. His own children had turned out alright. After all, neither Jessica's mother nor her father had managed to put the fear of God in their child's rebellious heart. He would be the one to do it. She surely had to be made to feel in the flesh, the deep concern, and care of those who loved her. It would only be for her own good.

Jessica winced hearing this. She could already feel her uncle's belt on her back. Shivering, she started to hug herself and rock back and forth. Grandmother Anne who had remained quiet the whole time indicated her desire to talk by a slight inflection of the hand. "Let us not forget in all this excitement that the child was not alone in that bathroom. She did not fornicate by herself. There was a man involved. Someone much older, whom I strongly believe, should bear the brunt of our wrath and the responsibility for this unfortunate incident and our child's expulsion from school. He preyed on the innocent and has wronged this family. What are you going to do about that man? And let us not forget, the child also has to be tested for pregnancy and diseases."

A few seconds felt like an eternity. No one talked for a while. Not of a mind to give Jessica a pass, or an easy way out.

"We certainly will be filing a complaint for child sexual abuse. After all, he raped her," Jessica's father said. His voice was thick with emotion. "The bastard went to her school, walked into the girls' bathroom with intent to harm, and assaulted Jessica, knowing full well she's a minor!"

All agreed. Jessica opened her mouth. "That's not true!"

"What's wrong, dear?" said the grandmother.

"He did not rape me."

"Hush child. You don't know what you're saying," her mother said. "Do you have the hots for that disgrace of a man?"

Jessica was adamant. "He's my boyfriend."

"You don't know the law, child. You don't know anything. Hush." Her mother rebuked.

"I don't care!"

"Do you have no sense at all? His name, give us his name, right this instant!"

At the High School and the Middle School next door, Jessica is all anyone talked about all week: how a girl had been found engaged in intercourse with a mechanic twice her age in the old gym's toilets. At the Middle School, the staff was in disbelief. Teachers there knew Jessica well. It could not be; it had to be a mistake!

She'd been an outstanding student, a caring, and considerate soul, not one of those good-for-nothings, you could already tell were going to throw their lives away. A star student, she had been their pride and joy, and teachers wanted to be of some support to the family in this time of difficulty.

Kirby, Jessica's former math teacher, took the initiative to write and send a most gracious note joined to a card signed by all of her former Middle School teachers with statements of support. They would do anything to help the family. Anything!

Kirby made sure to mention an alternative public school located outside of town in a repurposed church compound where Jessica may be able to complete High School among girls who had strayed, and became mothers prematurely.

Usually cold and distant, that act of kindness was uncharacteristic of Kirby. He had a reputation for being stingy, with money, good grades, his time, compliments and praises. He never seemed to care all that much for people. On occasions, when out with co-workers, to be a good sport, when others ordered a beer, Kirby would order water with lemon to join them in the merrymaking and clinking of glasses. He nibbled on lettuce and free bread and then told anyone that wanted to hear it, he was on a diet.

No one remembered ever seeing Kirby pay for anything other than an occasional cup of coffee. He'd refuse to pick up the tab for anything pricier, anyway. He looked dapper and was conscious of his flawless appearance— and most people dismissed him as 'in the closet.' Kirby was a likable bore.

A polished and memorable fellow, he wore to great effect the fashionable multicolored clothes he bought in thrift stores in upscale neighborhoods. Paying more than ten dollars for a pair of slacks and last season's fashion felt like an aberration. He'd remove the yellow from not-so-white-shirts with slight doses of bleach in the hot cycle of a machine wash. He'd never spend more than ten dollars for high-quality cotton shirts either.

Numbers were his thing ever since Grandpa had sat him on his lap, dangerously close to his crotch, and let TV educate them both on the value of money and compound interest. Fascinated with money, everything in Kirby's world revolved around it; the power it held over people's lives, and what it made possible.

An educator, Kirby saw numbers everywhere and knew the exact cost of the littlest indulgence. As a kid, insisting on candy meant there could not be extra coins for the collection plate on Sunday at church. Money held tremendous power on the mood of everyone in his household.

When the government check arrived, arguments were put on hold, and Joy made a temporary comeback. Mom and dad sat down after payday, spent more happy time together and shared meals as normal people do. Payday held a magical spell.

"Should I call and risk angering him?"

Jessica wanted to talk to the 'mechanic.' She could no longer keep her pain to herself. A phone call might be too risky. Everyone was looking for him and probably spying on her every move. She had to be careful. If at home his wife overheard the conversation, it would be game over. Phone calls were easy to trace too. Records could be summoned in court. At the very least, there would be a bill with the details of whom called whom.

No, she shouldn't call.

Instead, she would go to him and talk face to face. But how? He had been clear, and they were never to meet away from school. He also had to be the one who initiated contact. There was too much at stake. He'd refused to rely on the savvy of a sixteen-year-old. How could she possibly meet him now that she'd been expelled? However, he had to know!

She would not face this alone. Maybe he'd be able to tell her what to do! That's it! She'd go to his car. She knew where to find it most times. She'd throw onlookers off by leaving a note under ten other car windshield wipers, including his, and then wait nearby. The note would have the secret code that identified her, xoxoxo, and a message: "I want to make a home with you. I'm pregnant."

No one could find out his secret. The old woman would be the only exception. He trusted her to keep quiet. He'd used her services before. He'd done nothing wrong.

Love is not a crime.

He'd destroy anything and anyone that got in the way of his happiness. He removed the money from the pocket of his dirty uniform, and the old disheveled wiry hag, an Obeah woman, took it surreptitiously, without counting.

She placed it in her apron, yawned, and then let out almost in a whisper, 'morrow.'

The anguished wait would soon be over. She would hand over a miraculous bottle. The bush doctor looked like she consorted with the spirits of slaves. Her sullen demeanor gave off an otherworldly feel. She came from a different time; when being seen or heard spelled your doom, and invisibility was the best guarantor of survival in relative dignity.

Feared for what she knew and for whom she'd become, no one felt foolish enough to dare look her in the eyes. It was said, those eyes could stunt your brain and kill your spirit. Their intense focus pierced through insecurities. With a face sunken in gravity, burrowed by deep resilience, she had nursed many other people's fears. The sullen woman wielded a power rooted in studied assurance; she slowly turned away as if to bid her farewell.

Jessica wondered what secrets had the plants revealed to the old woman? Why did people believe that she held the key to their better tomorrow, that dry little mother of an unknowable and unassailable faith?

Jessica pinched her nose and drank the potion as instructed, a mixture of wild pineapple and a weed called pompon boiled in pungent crimson wine. A glass a day, preferably on an empty stomach. How had the Obeah woman known the right dosage?

After securely tucking away his borrowed mechanics' uniform under the front passenger seat of the car, Kirby, Jessica's boyfriend made his way home. He soon passed the threshold of the rental apartment where he lived with his younger brother's wife, his younger brother freshly returned from Afghanistan, and their dog.

He'd allowed them to stay until he found a job and got back on his feet. They had fallen on hard times. He'd told them they could stay however long it took. The stench of fried food, the racket of loud conversations competing with an unwatched TV on at full blast and the unrelenting dog barks of a pit bull terrier assaulted his senses and disquieted his mind. He wanted to scream.

He wanted to process everything that had happened recently and decide on the way forward with Jessica. He needed to think; and felt an urge to bring order to the dysfunctional scene. His brother's wife feared the worse. She quickly left the room, upon seeing his frown and disgruntled mug.

She remembered too well how volatile the two brothers could be. They insulted each other. The three-story complex was an outrage to urban architecture, but the rent remained affordable, so no one complained too vigorously. Tempers flared out of control, and the two men escalated the altercation by pushing and shoving, trying to provoke a full on fight. They almost came to blows. A neighbor's warning of his call to the police quieted down the situation and caused the younger brother and his wife to take a long walk outside to cool it for the evening. It was either that or spending the night in jail.

"I know you think you can handle your brother, but I can't. I've had enough of him. I've had enough of this whole situation. Let's go to my parents.' We'll make the best of it as long as we have each other."

After getting into it with his brother, he was now facing his wife's anger.

"Honey, I'm not gonna find a job in that small town. There's nothing going on there. We need to be here, in the big city where everything happens. My big break's gonna come from here. I've got a lead for a job in security. They'll call soon."

"If this job doesn't pan out, promise me, we'll go."

"I can't do that, hon'. We'll just have to wait and see."

"I don't like this!"

Feeling ignored by a man she thought was hers, that she suspected was putting more distance between them; cut off from her peers; stuck at home most of the time under her family's watchful eyes; driven to madness by the scrutiny; tired of being given the run-around and of the nagging thought of having been a pawn in a grown man's sick fantasy, a game she didn't remember signing up for, Jessica decided to call. She had made up her mind and wanted his wife to find out about the affair, hoping she'd finally leave him, making room for her.

"Why am I the only one to suffer? What did I ever do to you that was so wrong? Why are you joining forces with everyone in wanting to punish me? I read the card."

Kirby's brother was not supposed to hear the recorded messages. Too late! Sucked in, he allowed his curiosity to get the better of him, and listened in. The last message left on the answering machine shook him.

"My periods have come back. They look strange, though. Lumpy and pungent. Something, I'm sure, must have flushed." Jessica knew she wasn't supposed to reach out to him at home; that doing so could compromise his home life, but she did it anyway. She was desperately expecting a response about them moving in together. "Apparently, the weird-looking medicine we bought worked, I think. When will I see you again, Kirby?"

Could it be? The unsteady voice was that of a child. The soldier felt his blood boil. Distraught and incredulous, he resolved to confront his brother that very evening.

Kirby told the police his brother had been swinging a knife in his face, and described an unprovoked attack followed by an accidental defensive stabbing. All he had wanted to do was to protect himself. He claimed to love his brother and have no malice toward him. He was willing to do anything to make things right.

"I didn't want to hurt him. He's short-tempered and takes everything to the extreme."

"He's been like that, intense and scary, since he returned from Afghanistan."

The brother's wife said that she was climbing the stairs when she heard a commotion and rushed upstairs to see what the yelling was all about. It happened all the time.

When she came into the room, she found her husband moaning convulsively in a thick pool of blood, drifting in and out of consciousness.

"Kirby was by his side crying inconsolably, like a child, next to a blood-soaked kitchen knife on the floor."

She immediately left him to call 911. That night, from the living room, the police recovered two weapons, a Swiss army knife and a kitchen knife. An answering machine whose cord had been savagely pulled from its socket on the wall lied smashed on the floor. Kirby's sister in law cursed the day she'd agreed to move into the apartment; she had sensed there would be trouble. There'd always been trouble between those two. Her husband didn't make it. He died in the ambulance. Shortly afterward, the police booked Kirby for manslaughter.

His secret was safe for now. He would be anything, except a pedophile.

RUMBLE

His gait singled him out. He could be seen meandering in the streets of Pointe-à-Pitre, stopping only to join groups of young men assembled by the side of the road, sometimes on street corners.

Unlike the locals, Longineu walked straight, looking ahead unconcerned with what others might be thinking. He listened to people's rage in this time of grave political unrest, work stoppages, barricades, general strikes and youth rebellions against the Establishment. Patrice first saw Longineu in Raizet, a neighborhood in a high-density area, in the city of Abymes. The saxophone case hanging from his shoulder made him look innocent.

What threat would a musician pose? he reckoned. If he got mad, people would dance.

Most locals thought nothing of Longineu.

There were so many artists in these parts. He looked just like the rest of them. Another nappy-headed, happy-go-lucky musician. A bespectacled high yellow dude of average stature sporting a 'fro.

He seemed well into his thirties. His slight frame, average looks, and ordinary features prompted no one to take a second glance at him. The jeans and T-shirts he wore helped him blend in with the crowds. His leisurely attitude and dress style made him seem carefree and approachable, almost friendly. Patrice didn't believe anyone on the streets had yet heard his voice then. The saxophone player listened and nodded, smiled a lot when others smiled, mimicked them when they gestured, but weaseled out whenever someone too forward took an interest in talking with him. If he hadn't, they'd have discovered his secret. Longineu was all about the word on the street.

Patrice watched Longineu and wondered about the man. Poker-faced, emotionless, yet always present. The man was a mystery who haunted Patrice's thoughts.

Didn't he have anything else to do? Like, take cover. Who the hell was he? And what was he really looking for?

Drawn in by Patrice's inquisitive stares, Longineu greeted him with a bob of the head.

The puny kid was no threat, Longineu thought. Just an island fixture that popped up wherever he happened to be. A bored ragamuffin in search of excitement, no doubt; come to think of it; and school was out.

In Guadeloupe, Longineu would pay four to five times more than in the States. A two-liter bottle of Coke would be $4, instead of 99 cents. A simple hamburger would be $6, instead of the two dollars he was used to paying. Economic disparities and structural inequalities plagued the French Antilles and French Guiana. The collapse of agriculture had left many unemployed.

Unemployment was three times higher than in France. There was a 50% unemployment rate for those under twenty-five who made up over half the overall population. Agricultural production gave way to a service economy centered on tourism, commerce, and a bloated government bureaucracy. The economy was on its knees.

As a little boy, every Wednesday, Patrice opened his piggy bank to retrieve the precious coins he'd been saving. Those he had collected from the deep recesses of the armchair. They had fallen out of his father's pants while he would fall asleep. The old man would have no use for them now. He'd needed them for a tip here and there.

In the course of a day's work, in his cash register, Patrice's father would collect wads of bills. So Patrice thought, what difference would a few missing coins make?

Sometimes too, his mother would hand him a generous amount of her own coins right before driving him to their favorite kiosk where he would purchase the latest editions of the comic books he liked so much, Zembla, Hakim and the likes. The scantily clad heroes depicted in the magazines, the kings of the African jungle were all white.

As a boy, he'd been taught that the world belonged to white men, dressed and undressed, because they had answers to everything, their might knew no bounds, and they always made sense.

American Indians, Aboriginal peoples, Asians, and Africans made no sense, even when they tried, victims of their own magical thinking and lack of military strength. As mere props in someone else's game, they existed to serve at the white man's whim.

Patrice's own schooling had reinforced the lies. It had sought to make him a handy tool. Gratitude remained the only fitting response he was ever allowed to give an army of benevolent usurpers.

The French believed their domination to be a blessing to a lesser people. The colonialists strove daily to set the natives' souls free of the profound darkness they claimed entrapped them. Patrice was learning his place. The lesson of his insignificance was taking root.

"Hey man. How are you? I keep seeing you wherever I turn."

"I'm alright. You're the one I keep seeing everywhere I turn. Are you some kind of a reporter?"

"No man, just curious."

"You're clearly not from the Caribbean. Your accent gives you away. Where are you from?"

"I'm from Georgia. The name's Longineu."

"Mine's Patrice. The U.S.? That's a first. All the tourists are gone! What brings you here at a time like this?"

Longineu laughed. "Oh, well. I came with my wife. She's doing research on traditional Guadeloupian culture and dance, and refuses to leave. She has a dance studio here. Before Guadeloupe, we lived in Senegal for a while. She was also doing research, on Senegalese folk culture. The black world's fascinating to us.

We're artists. When we return home, we'll incorporate what we've learned."

"Senegal, uh?"

Longineu smiled. "Yes. Senegal is a wonderful and vibrant country. Its youth is smart, creative, and beautiful. A lack of resources does nothing to deter the inventiveness of its people. They're proud, gentle and elegant, despite the dire poverty. Much like your people, they displayed no ill feelings toward us. Communicating with them was generally pleasant."

The saxophone player paused and looked around the streets, a small smile pursed his lips. "After a while, we just couldn't take living there any longer. Getting around Dakar was difficult; taxicabs felt unsafe. No one respected the rules of the road; Wolof interfered with our ability to learn French; power outages; constant begging on the streets; all of this created a huge inconvenience. As if this wasn't enough, men boldly accosted and offered to marry my wife; a huge source of daily irritation. We got sick often, and so we decided to move closer to home and ended up here in Guadeloupe. These trips have opened my eyes to the black world outside of the States."

"Are you not aware of what's going on here

these days?" Patrice frowned.

"I know what's going on, even though the televised news doesn't help much. I try to go where people are, so I can learn more. There's so much more info on the street. My French is not very good and sometimes it's challenging to make out what people say. And if that wasn't hard enough, many among you break into Creole, or mix it up way too much for my taste. I miss a lot of what's said." The man bit his lip and looked at him.

"Since you follow me around, could you help out on occasions?"

"I don't follow you around. You showed up in my town. Remember! Help with what? What do you need?"

What American does that, look for poorer places to move to? Patrice wondered. Normal people look for comfort. Longineu had to be up to no good. Why did he even pick me to explain and translate what was hard for him to get? Sure, they taught English in school, but how did he know for sure I even speak the language, in a land where French is king? Was he kidding?

The boy was seventeen. He wondered if the saxophone player knew who he was dealing with. Most foreigners, especially Americans, never mingled with the locals, and instead remained secluded in beach resorts.

To be an American is to cultivate fear, to be shaped by fear. Americans hardly ever came to these shores. When they came at all, the tourists traveled in packs or stayed cloistered in air-conditioned tour buses and hotel rooms. They loafed around white sandy beaches, or stayed on board showy cruise ships and continued on.

Longineu was itching to ask a question he sensed was too sensitive. He'd opened up enough and felt entitled anyway.

"Patrice, do you know anyone involved in the unrest?"

The suspicious son of a separatist, Patrice was of a mind to play a trick on Longineu.

"Yeah. Only four. They placed bombs in a few locations too."

"Who are they?"

"One of them is a nurse. Another, a doctor. Another, an architect, and I can't recall what the last one did for a living."

"You seem pretty plugged in. How do you know these people?"

"This is a small island, man. We all practiced karate together. They are my elders."

"How can I meet them? I'd love to ask a few questions. Popular liberation movements fascinate me. It's almost like I'm part of history right now."

"So, you're into swinging and kinky stuff, uh?"

The man looked at him and blinked. "What?"

"These guys, uh, you know, they are... They're all dead. They blew up with their bombs. Premature detonation."

Longineu and Patrice crossed paths again. No one talked. Relentless, he was still out there hanging out with the youths, but he no longer approached. He'd resented being mocked by the cheeky teenager. Longineu had gotten nothing useful out of Patrice who kept watching him. He saw him lurk in dark alleys like a pusher of death, and noticed the snitches feeding at his hand. After meeting with Longineu, they always had a little pep in their step and money to impress silly girls.

One day, children stopped hanging out on street corners and classes resumed. On Wednesday, class let out early. Half a day of freedom was a welcome break in a hectic week spent playing catch-up at school. A demanding national curriculum weighed on the minds of the ambitious students who wanted a ticket off of the island. The Baccalauréat was that ticket.

Patrice devoted the best part of Wednesday afternoons to relieving the anxiety associated with the end-of-year examination. After lunch, he left Baimbridge High, took a detour instead of heading straight home, dodged in and out of traffic, and made his way to the international airport in Raizet, his favorite place to hang out. There, he took a seat opposite the departure gate that led to customs and a security screening.

Patrice gawked at the departing travelers; detailed their accouterments, pictured the types of exciting lives they led in the faraway places where hope resided. He imagined that one day, he would be lucky enough to join them. Home would be anywhere, but here. The French colony was a jail for a restless soul. His land was under siege, bleeding faith.

Every time Patrice saw Longineu's wife, Beverly, she inspired a second look. A tall sleek brown skin beauty, all sugar and spice and everything nice. Her syncopated moves delighted all who watched. Everyone in town had borne witness to her gift. She floated like a hummingbird hugging the frenzied air. The tussle she called a dance riveted onlookers. Hearts throbbed with every thrust of her quivering limbs.

On the street, in the studio, anywhere there was a beat, a mere sound, a vibration, a flutter, she would engage in a modern and stylish convulsion unlike any seen before. The dreadful trance was a celebration of life. The dance invoked ancestors, wandering spirits and lost souls denied heaven or hell.

Beverly delivered an otherworldly performance she called modern dance, while the profane called it a pageantry of madness. It was her singular interpretation of what local culture meant to her. She communicated loud and clear, reminding the audience to honor from whence they'd come. Contorting to imaginary blows, her emotions became their pain.

The American woman understood them. She embodied their resistance to the theft of their spirit. She became one with Guadeloupe, gave the land her all. Beverly had a finger on the pulse of the island. She'd become one of them.

The revival of Creole language and Gwo Ka music and dance brought people together to feed the flame of nationalism.

Patrice had followed Longineu for weeks before school resumed. He'd sought to expose him. Discreet, steering clear of Main Street, Longineu disappeared into alleyways only the locals knew, then, like a ghost, reappeared where no one expected him. Curious, Longineu asked lots of questions to the people he flattered. Adept at building rapport with public figures and low-life felons equally, he placed himself on anyone's level for the occasion, adopting their taste in a subtle show of conciliation.

When he'd open up to someone, his fanciful stories would lighten up their face inspiring admiration. Like an opportunist, he jumped at any chance to obtain the scoop he wanted. At times, cautious in the extreme, not wanting to show his hand, when the tide shifted, and people doubted his motivation, he backed off, played dumb and made his exit. No one was none the wiser. He got along with assholes and decent folk alike. Getting others to talk came naturally to him.

His undeniable strength, listening, paid dividends. Popular with the natives, they extended invitations to places tourists never visited. Rumor had it; he'd been seen at the hideout of a notorious drug dealer, sitting on the ground, eating red beans and rice from a calabash, his signature musical instrument lying flat on a bench nearby. During the carnival, he and Beverly were the first to break ranks with staid onlookers standing dignified on the sidewalk. They would lunge into the booming chaos of disorderly flesh partaking in unbridled popular hysteria in the middle of the streets.

Guadeloupe had always been a battlefield, a pawn in the interplay of the greed and envy of powerful interests; a playground for rich Europeans manicured by poor West Indians. Culture and identity are on everyone's mind in Guadeloupe. Anti-colonialist sentiments felt commensurate to the harsh treatment the locals received at the hands of the French. Guadeloupe doesn't feel or look like France. It is America. It may, at times, remind one of France, but it is warm, lush, hilly, tiny and mostly languid; unless, of course, in the throes of a deep-seated anger that like the thick slow-moving lava from the Soufriere volcano, stews just beneath the surface ready to burst at the slightest irritation.

The dissatisfaction with the status quo led to the rise of a virulent anticolonial movement. In the eighties, a strong nationalist wave of bombings, riots, and unrest rocked the archipelago. General strikes provided an effective response to state oppression. The first bomb attack occurred in 1983, and the last, in 1985. Sixty bombings took place in the archipelago, in Martinique, in French Guiana, and in France, targeting banks, hotels, luxury stores like Chanel, airline companies, automobile clubs, police stations, prisons, tax offices, and restaurants. Spray-painted slogans that read "French People Out" appeared and multiplied all over the walls of cities.

In Guadeloupe, you would not find the filth and chaotic resignation found in Haiti nor the abysmal desperation found in Jamaica. You would only find the madness brought about by multiple identities, split personalities warring against each other, a living legacy of the abuses perpetrated in the flesh and in the soul of a people, in the name of French civilization.

Reminiscent of the flag of Suriname, the large green-red-green UPLG flag, a white stripe between the green and the red, and a bright yellow five pointed star to the left fluttered frantically and led a procession of rambunctious overloaded cars to a far-off conference hall down at the mouth of Hell. There, in the wilderness, the people of the soil assembled in an unpretentious building to await their leader.

The strong man appeared at last. The rumblings subsided. He looked as dark as their pain and as large as their aspirations. His dark hue made him a compelling son of the same fertile soil, ready for a new crop, a rebirth of the spirit. Doctor Makouke hovered above a packed audience moved by the single-minded obsession of removing the yoke of the usurper masquerading as a friend, jolly and benevolent.

Endorphins inundated Patrice's brain. Flanked by his mother and his aunt, protected by the fervor of patriots, comrades in the struggle for the sovereignty of their common will, Patrice marveled at the big man shattering the silence.

For the best part of an hour, he delivered a mesmerizing harangue the likes of which Patrice had never heard.

Doctor Makouke's power didn't just come from his booming voice, or his unmistakable presence, it came from the profundity of his convictions, which married to everyone else's, charged the air. Prodded by revolutionary zeal, a procession of cars in the thousands crawled to the barricades outside of Pointe-à-Pitre.

Since early morning, restless patriots had heeded the call to protest the arbitrary rule of the enforcers of inequity. They needed assistance. To the rescue, the guardians of the soil went like an army of Mau Mau warriors on the prowl to prolong the resistance for a few additional hours.

Against sticks and stones, the khakied-reactionary troops of well-paid government terrorists rained down tear gas sending protesters blindly scurrying for cover into tenement yards, back alleys, and the improvised shelter of welcoming shacks.

Water splashed on the sullied faces of women and children gasping for air provided relief and the undeterred were ready once again to face their tormentors.

For weeks on end after the Doctor's speech, Longineu roamed the streets looking for evidence of discontent, until all talks quieted, groups disbanded, and normalcy returned stilling and sending all rumblings to pasture. The marches and the bombings stopped, the streets emptied, and life resumed its predictable steady pace. The children returned to their soccer games, and the old, to their liquor parlors where sugar and lime mixed again, happy to greet the fragrant local rum.

One day, without warning, Longineu disappeared. He was gone, nowhere to be found, never to be seen again. The dance studio closed permanently. There was no longer any point to watching half-hidden behind shutters, hoping to spot his frail shadow. He was gone. No point in considering spying on his every deceptive move, or in trailing him mindlessly under cover of darkness to the back of unmarked police cars where his steps always led once the angry crowds dispersed.

The gendarmes came for Patrice early one

morning and parked in front of the family home. He wondered how they knew he'd be home alone. He watched them through the twilight induced by the plantation shutters. The pit in his stomach would not let him breathe. The huge gendarme truck with rows of open benches in the rear held fifteen officers; lifelike robots made of flesh.

Under the rising sun their alabaster skin turned red, making them uncomfortable in their fatigues; in their hands, the heavy machinery of death; they were chomping at the bits to launch into action. The struggle for liberation at that moment seemed excruciatingly real. Were they about to rob Patrice of his body, or trample his spirit? Hostage to the whim of a higher up, no one moved. The implacable fear growing within Patrice became heart-rending.

Awaiting an order, the dealers of death could not leave the truck. Like a moth, Patrice stayed glued to the shutters, expecting their actions to dictate his fate, resisting the urge to urinate. The pain shooting from his bladder to the tip of his penis sharpening. The truck started suddenly, reawakening his dread, and took off in a huff with its guns and trained hands.

In the wake of Longineu's unexplained

departure, street-corner activists' imprisonment swiftly followed. Returning from a date at the movies, a high school student with whom Patrice sometimes played soccer was stopped and frisked by an impatient gendarme who demanded to see his papers. The student had often been seen bantering with the American. He failed to promptly produce his identification. Multiple detonations rang out, and he fell hard like a lump to the ground.

Seventeen years old, motionless on a slimy bed of asphalt, the victim of cowardly, uncaring, government bullets, dead; a casualty of the fear of the usurper. Was this the price one had to pay for a fraudulent peace? The loss of the seed of a brighter future? That colonial peace robbed real people of the hope of dignity and the dream of finally owning their bodies.

Patrice would never again speak to random tourists, outsiders from the North, mingling with locals in times of unrest. Unaffected, Longineu had been more afraid than most, while no violence had been directed at him or his family or his country; not the violence of colonial domination nor the retaliation of the dominated. Longineu was as safe as he wanted to be, always a plane ticket away from ultimate safety.

He was safe if he wanted to be, unlike the natives who had nowhere else to run. He could leave and regain his shores anytime. Because of his quest and dealings, he'd made smelling fear his stock in trade; he could only be a spy. How else could Patrice explain Longineu's infatuation with and the pursuit of drama? He had to have been a spy. Patrice had suspected this much the moment he'd appeared on the scene. How else could the unexpected targeted arrests and the murder of his acquaintance be explained?

Communists hung around high schools, and like Mormons and Jehovah's witnesses, they traveled in pairs using gimmicks to grab the attention of impressionable young people to teach them the ways of their enemies. The colorful material donated by Cuba railed against American and European imperialism, highlighting the spiritual wickedness of takers and bloodsuckers, those who sanctified the "I," elevated it most highly.

They warned against people like Longineu who were doing the Devil's work for a pittance they called a living, identified as they were with their master's cause. The communists trained the youth in how to monitor evil, in the name of a God they called Liberation. Patrice would no longer shun them.

He saw them again, the night before, hovering about his place, playing with his fears. He thought it strange they stayed so long this time, and when they left, with a smile, they looked his way through the shutters, one last time. The next day, they came for him, this time, in earnest. They stopped by the class he was in, with people that knew him.

They made a school administrator fetch him, interrupt the bonding, and deliver him in a cold corridor dressed the color of despair. Intent on bruising his flesh, they assaulted his resigned, motionless body. They tackled and restrained him; tightly shackled his hands and hauled him into the belly of their gaping monster of steel.

They drove slowly around the school, doing a victory lap for all to see, as his defeated soul sank into a hopeless silence. Patrice had never been arrested before, much less humiliated in such a public fashion. Of what was he accused exactly? Why? It didn't much matter! He was born accused, guilty and condemned; lacking a sovereign will. His body and soul trapped in the lust and fears of others; soul on ice. Half-crazed, waiting for his father, Patrice faded into compulsive reverie. The murdered high school student spoke to him:

"Beware! Deceit, lies, theft, are all around.

A spy's perfidy is revealed when you refuse to entertain the tale he weaves. In the details, he'll show his hand. Too much 'I,' not enough 'we.' He'll talk too much or not enough, and way too carefully. He'll be too nice, or not at all. Watch the veneer fade and his true colors emerge. Keep a distance. Nothing good ever comes of engaging with trolls. Trust your instincts. A suspicion is all you need. Run. A troll cares only for himself, and shows up in your life uninvited like spam. Delete, and turn inward, where your truth resides. Do not open yourself to a lie and a bullet."

On the high school student's grave, Patrice emptied a heavy heart.

DISRUPTION

Lester needed to know whether his mother was alright. She was supposed to have returned home to Saint John's, Antigua, from a recent visit to her youngest son in Philipsburg, Sint Maarten. For the last four weeks, Lester had been without news of either.

He used to love to visit Kenneth on the 13-square-mile Dutch island of 34,000 inhabitants. Sint Maarten had more gaming machines per resident than any other country in the world. Kenneth's sudden wealth, the rumors of money laundering and cocaine trading, all convinced Lester he should stay away from his little brother till he could figure out what was going on.

Mostly, he wanted to gloat over his newfound bliss. Lester wanted his mother to know how right she'd been, Marilyn was a keeper.

Traffic was slow in the suburbs of Washington, DC. The bus sputtered along heaving through a campus the size of a small town toward the old complex, five miles away, where he lived with his bride. All Lester had ever wanted in life was a good marriage. And being in love was only a plus.

Life was good. Intact families were hard to come by where he came from. No one in his circle of family and friends enjoyed anything resembling a steady relationship. He did what no other man he knew had done; he'd settled down and broken the curse.

Exhausted, and eager to make it back to their one-bedroom love nest, he'd call his mother first and then, cuddle up with the love of his life. After a long day at work, a snuggle helped them relax.

Without as much as a jingle from the keys, Lester opened the door to the cushy living room where the house phone rested, covered in darkness. No waft of a home-cooked meal was coming from the kitchen; there was no sign of life in the sleepy apartment. Maybe Marilyn was stuck at work again. That only meant one thing, he would be the one fixing dinner tonight.

In the stillness of his residence, he picked up the receiver preparing to dial. Coming from the phone, before he could press the first key, he made out the voice of a man. The man's voice had a tone he had never heard before. Piqued, Lester's fingers slipped as he focused, pricked his ears and listened to the stranger's voice.

"Leave him. Come with me instead. I'll take care of you." And then, a woman's. Marilyn's voice, he was sure!

"No, I can't leave him. I just married the man. I can't leave."

Lester breathed in sharply. His stomach twisted and he felt like he was going to throw up. Blood started flooding his brain. His nostrils flared, his chest tightened. Struggling to retain his wits about him, he felt like hollering. A sharp pain shot through his lungs. Listening carefully offered the best defense against a rush to judgment. There was no room for error with what he was fixing to do. After five agonizing minutes, exasperated with the silly banter, back and forth, "Leave him," "No, I won't," Lester slammed the phone down so hard he broke it. Then he heard a gasp and smelled anguish coming from the bedroom. He'd heard things he wasn't supposed to hear. That much she knew!

In disbelief, Marilyn wanted to cover herself with the blanket, instead she tried to perk up from the California king size where she'd been lying half-naked, curled up against a down pillow. Her eyes widened and she braced for a violent confrontation. Eyes now round with frenzied anticipation, alert and upright, she jolted throwing the duvet to the floor.

Lester stormed into the room. His stout frame, reminiscent of a quarterback's, filled the bedroom door frame and she suddenly cowered like a battered woman, drained of any inclination to engage in a fight she could not win. He watched angrily as his wife shrank into the bed, making herself look smaller than she already was. Seeking mercy. He hardened his gaze, while she softened hers. Eventually, Lester looked at her and saw her flinch and knew that he was the cause of her fear. Shaking his head, he sat down at the edge of the bed and stared at the wall. He tried to take several breaths to calm himself down. In the heavy silence, a sharp coldness descended into the room.

Lester's baby face, square jaw, large forehead, and burning eyes reminded her of why she loved him. She relaxed. He got up violently. She dropped the bedroom phone to her feet and made herself so small again, even her breasts appeared scrunched; her mouth was agape, she was preparing for an abusive rant from a man she had never meant to anger. She loved him! Menacingly, Lester stepped closer to the bed. Marilyn backed all the way up to the headboard, then let herself slide on the bed where the pillow met the board, lifting her arms as if to defend against a blow. Witnessing the dread he had inspired, Lester froze, then sat down again quietly at the foot of the bed in a reluctant gesture of appeasement, keeping a stern lock on her lowered gaze. Hurt, vexed, full of rage, at that moment a gulf separated them, threatening to tear asunder a bond she had made fragile. She spoke first.

"Lester, I love you, honey. I said no. Did you hear me say, no?"

"You said no. Why did you have to say it so many times? Why did you have to say it at all?"

"I said no. That is all that matters!"

"Maybe to you. Had he not had our number, you wouldn't have had to say anything at all."

"I said no, honey. I don't want anyone other than my husband."

"I'm glad I was here just in time to hear this, because now I know you're no good. Not good enough for me anyway. You're not the lady I thought you were." Marilyn reached for him, but he shrugged her off.

"Why can't you hear me? What is it I did that was so wrong?"

"I think you should go, woman. If you don't know, I got no time to 'splain it to you. Nothing else to say to you. Leh me lone."

"Honey, please. I haven't done anything wrong. I met that guy at work. We became friends. Nothing happened, I swear."

"Okay, I hear you. All the same, I can't trust you. I think you get that already."

"You're making a mistake honey. Please, don't…"

"How long has this been going on? He asks you to leave your husband. What made him feel it was okay to even ask you that? Oh, I know. It was you. Your attitude. Please go. Me nah like um."

No longer in the mood for eating or calling his mother, Lester grabbed the duvet off the floor, then went to the living room to crash on the large sofa. He spent every night shriveled up in the fetal position that week lamenting the time, money and effort he wasted on someone undeserving of his love and commitment. How could he have been so blind and so stupid? She was a knockout, but he was the one left feeling the pain.

It hadn't been six months since the wedding ceremony. An annulment was still an option. What had gone wrong? What had he done wrong? He had waited so long to find the perfect woman. How could a reserved, family-oriented, so tastefully put together, God-fearing woman with the face of an angel sink so low?

He thought about her. Her body, her lips, her smile and the way she would ride him each night. Lester thought she loved him and never figured she would try and deceive him.

Stepping into the bedroom each morning to retrieve the clothes he needed that day, seeing Marilyn's lascivious body spread bare onto the bed greeting his manhood, inviting a reconciliation felt like salt on a fresh wound. The firmness of her shapely body, the sweet caramel appeal of her skin, the taunting fullness of her perky breasts jogged his memory of better days, before he knew how low she could go. Knowing was punishment enough. To jump on top of her while she lay, launch a frontal attack to avenge the outrage, take the mound of Venus surrendered for solace, and do with it as he pleased, abuse it, chastise it with all the fury he could corral, pounce on it and then discharge with tremendous animus, and finally, allow calm to return; no, that would be capitulation to evil. An easy way out, undeserved absolution, for the sullied, and unworthy. She needed to suffer and feel the pain she had caused him.

Lester too had courted temptation at work, she wasn't the only one, but he did it only with his eyes and chose to hold his tongue; no words were ever exchanged; no action followed. He would do nothing to precipitate his downfall. Being married to a queen was that important to him. He'd even shut his treacherous eyes when the lure of another woman's flesh got to be too much to bear, until the rush of lust dissipated. By allowing a predator in the sacred space of their intimacy, by toying with the profane, Marilyn had ruined the magic. Lester no longer imagined himself unique. Marilyn no longer seemed special to him, either. They became ordinary, and in his eyes, she even turned ugly.

His dream of marriage had been stolen. He was a child of the curse. Who did he think he was anyway? How could he forget that he was the child of a family of broken hearts?

The dream of domestic bliss, being best friends with his spouse, having fun, enjoying time together, reveling in the comfort of knowing you have a safe place to fall was not to be for Lester; instead, a familiar dysfunction was beckoning like an old wretched low down and dirty friend. Who did he think he was anyway? How could he forget he was the child of his mother, and the grandchild of his grandmother? A long line of godforsaken people who had witnessed thieves steal their joy, along with the heart of a beloved. A child of the curse. Now, he too was getting acquainted with a thief. That was one thing, but another entirely to aid the thief by relinquishing his possession. Once despair reared its head, hope left. Lester lost his faith. Marilyn wasn't his to stop. Once the robbery occurred, once the incident with Marilyn occurred, he called his mother. He still remembered to worry about her. She'd always been there for him.

At work, his classes and students moved along predictably well. He was a seasoned instructor, one to whom students thronged when offered a choice. They enjoyed that he focused on their person, really listened. Every day Lester gave his all and left work spent. He needed the distraction now more than ever. To take his mind off the shambles he called his marriage, he needed that stage more than most. It kept him sane!

Lester spent the rest of the week withstanding the morning enticements, which left Marilyn reeling. She'd never been ignored, neglected, humiliated, rejected in the flesh, in her soul, and despised like that at the core. Her husband's resounding dismissal of her stung. One day, leaving the comfort of his stage, Lester returned to what had been their sanctuary, and found it eviscerated. The sofa was gone, and so were the dressers and the bed! He was grateful his clothes and the television set that had cost so much remained. The toilet was clogged. Feeling wronged, Marilyn had escaped his ruthless, unforgiving pride to stem the disparagement of her morality. She sought to make him pay for cheapening their love and not believing in her loyalty.

Floating above the living room, unhinged, with a sense of unreality, all of a sudden Lester's mind started to race. He rushed out to the closest ATM to check their joint account. The money was gone, most of it, anyway. Marilyn had left him one hundred dollars, not a penny more, just enough to eat before payday.

That was payback. The savings gone, and so was his paycheck. Tiny though it was, she had a heart. Shoulders hunched, fighting shadows, Lester dragged what was left of himself back to the disemboweled apartment, mumbling words of despair under his breath. Crushed, he fancied himself singing the blues.

"How could she?"

Before the betrayal, he'd on occasion been lax with the nooky, neglecting his duties. But he'd had his reasons. Was the world conspiring to hold him down? The holes in the condoms stored in the medicine cabinet for one; hell-bent on having a baby, Marilyn had pricked them.

Starting a life without support of any kind, no real money to speak of, up in shit's creek, no paddle in sight, he'd hoped she would understand. It was the wrong time for a baby. Then he remembered he was the one who had asked her to leave. Could she not have guessed it was his hurt talking that day?

A hot-tempered Antiguan never stayed mad very long, but calms down quickly. Why did she go if she'd done nothing wrong? And why did she take all their money, to boot? He would call his mother in Antigua and only then start wallowing in self-pity. Without an audience self-pity never felt quite as good.

"Wah a gwarn son?"

"Mom. It's finally happened. The very thing I never wanted to happen. Marilyn left."

"Tap lie. Chupit boy. No funny. You jus' got married."

He'd been dumped. It sucked. He was keeping with a sinister tradition as the rightful son of a cursed family. At the end of the month, like clockwork, the rent would come due. The thing was, without Marilyn around to pay her share, Lester was screwed, bound to come short, even if he got paid on time. The paycheck was already spoken for.

There were other bills too. Like a madman, flipping through random classified ads, he made frantic calls, searching for that affordable room to rent, possibly in a different town where no one knew of his failure, yet close enough to campus.

A working-class neighborhood of small boxy red brick houses built in the 1950s would do in Hyattsville; a town scarred by foreclosures, where American Blacks, Whites, Hispanics, West Indians, Africans, and Asians, side by side, minded their own business.

"What is there to think about? You need a room. I'm offering you one."

Lester hesitated in front of a lanky, restless, sallow-complexioned, a tuft of blond hair on top of the head, white man in his early thirties, his would-be landlord, intent, even eager to get his hands on the measly sum of money he was asking for the large bedroom. Something didn't quite feel right. He was unsettled. He had come to a jarring realization. Standing in front of a glazed-eyed ungroomed sickly compulsive yawner, lost in some distant Shangri-La, made his skin crawl, and gnawed at him. Lester drew in a sharp breath. He could prove nothing, yet could not ignore the pit in his stomach, nor his intuition. That was all he had. He heard himself, to his dismay; promise the would-be landlord he would consider the offer, all the while thinking:

"Heroin. Are you kidding me?"

He decided to run as fast as possible, and as far away as he could. On the spot, Lester dashed out of the house like a man possessed, turning back on occasions to watch his back for fear a club would knock him over the head from behind.

With the end of the month fast approaching, Lester was in no position to pay the rent in full, and he needed money for food. The only solution was to hurry out of the one-bedroom apartment. He bought newspapers, scoured more classified ads, and prayed for his salvation. Then he came upon a small, but promising rooming house in a different working-class part of town, made of the same red bricks as the previous one. This house made him feel entirely different. He was not scared.

"Howdy. Ah, ya. You're a college instructor. I see. Good, good."

A middle-aged Indonesian man of small stature, a smile always at the ready, the landlord liked that Lester worked at the local university. He didn't make much money, yet the landlord respected an educated man. He thought he would at least take better care of his investment than had the cook and the taxi driver occupying it.

Twenty-five years prior, the landlord, after moving his family to the United States, had lived in the small house. Now, he called home much more exclusive surroundings, far away from the riff-raff. He would not say where, afraid, maybe, the have-nots would disrupt his gated privacy. The rent represented only a fraction of what Lester was required to pay for the one-bedroom apartment, the Indonesian was not to find out Lester would be stiffing the old place.

There could be no ruined credit, no report, no record of what was to happen, at least not before the new lease was signed. Two days before the end of the month, for once happy to part with his money, Lester hurried and paid the new landlord.

Overcome with gratitude, he moved his clothes and the television-set into a large empty bedroom. Life was good again. A second lease, that's all he was asking for. He would survive, and eventually thrive. Little did he know then that, he and his estranged wife would not get away with not paying the money they owed? Months later, Lester begrudgingly settled the two remaining months on the former lease. Making the previous landlord whole was preferable to a damaged credit history. He bit the bullet. Money talked.

He did not see it coming! He took to slouching and dragging his feet to work. Showing up became an accomplishment. Depression was sneaky, and it slowly set in. Lester lost the cheerful disposition others had so loved about him. He held on, did his work, forged ahead and put on a decent face. He avoided women for an entire year, barely made eye contact, and turned down invitations to hang out.

Karen and Abby, two female colleagues of differing virtues, refused to give up on him. He was way too cute and "diggable to be left alone to sour in a lonely corner." A blind woman could tell, Lester needed a distraction.

Karen and Abby knew he liked what he saw when he had to look at them. The way he held his breath and the glimmer in his eyes gave it away each time. Why was he pretending not to care? They, like everybody else, knew his wife had left him for another man. Marilyn had made sure of it by never hiding. Karen and Abby wanted Lester. Letting a good thing go to waste, a tropical fruit so ripe was out of the question. They wanted a bite of him and would outdo each other to get him. It was on! Healthy flesh, unattended in plain sight, most unforgivable in Karen and Abby's starving world! Impervious to reason, unaware of the follies of his self-denial, Lester carried on like a eunuch. He was incorrigible! What West Indian man would turn down a perfectly good opportunity to indulge and let loose? He'd gone mad! Lester's misgivings about one woman had become his misgivings about all women.

Karen and Abby were attractive and young, like he was. And he'd been warned; they had a big crush on him. They liked that he made them feel fine. He listened to their banter even from a safe distance. Because of his eager, hungry eyes, they fancied themselves beautiful. They loved the way Lester looked at them. Tiring of waiting for him to make a move, they both, at different times, invited him to join in the fun at a birthday party here, or a night on the town there. Lester turned them down every time. He had lost confidence in himself.

One day, an outraged and exasperated African colleague, appalled by the lack of interest Lester showed in either woman, berated him for not taking up with one of the hotties.

"One day, no one will ask you out. You will be too old and too ugly. You are not a man. Can't you see these women want you? Hey, I even think Abby loves you. She's so sweet. In my country…"

How dare he question my manhood? Lester thought. He wouldn't get over the affront this easily. "You are not a man." What a thing to say to a hot-blooded West Indian!

If only to shut the African's trap, he resolved to have dinner with Abby. He'd give her a chance, even for no other reason. A dazzling sea green-eyed beauty, Abby was the most sensitive and thoughtful of the two, not as fiercely independent as the assertive and outgoing Karen who reminded him too much of Marilyn.

In the history department where they worked, Abby always demonstrated poise, good judgment, and a compelling intelligence at staff meetings. She knew when to keep quiet and when to speak up. She seemed predictable and consistent. On the surface she had everything going for her. She was smart, extroverted, gorgeous in an uncanny way. She seemed to believe she had to prove she wasn't the stupid, loud, affirmative action pick some people assumed she was. So she seldom raised her voice.

Always well-attired she kept an expensive professional wardrobe and made sure to remove any trace of a dialect in her speech. She wanted everyone to believe as she believed that she was excellent at her job. Any slight or criticism had the power to cause her to unravel and doubt herself.

With Lester, she felt whole. He understood her struggle. A fellow West Indian, with him she could indulge, let herself go and be seen as the island girl that she was, relishing callaloo, breadfruit "oil down," and calypso music without risking being judged and thought less of. She already loved Lester more than she loved herself. He favored her father. Around him, she felt safe and unconsciously reverted to being a needy little girl, not the assertive woman everyone knew her as.

Lester felt ready, and better off. He had a bed and a dresser now, and no longer looked destitute. He'd regained some control over his life. He'd even bought a used Volvo; a station wagon that ran well and took him from point A to point B, and most importantly, the marriage to Marilyn had long been annulled.

He called Abby prepared to kiss the blues goodbye. She would be available for takeoff at eight o'clock sharp. It was Friday. They'd go out on the town, have dinner, then be off to a trendy comedy club and maybe afterward, if they still cared for each other's company, to a dance club in Washington, DC. She was game. Anything could happen! One could never go wrong when laughter and movement were involved.

A lady and a gentleman, both on their best behavior, they sought to charm each other's pants off. Abby was a svelte 5"7, 128 pounds, toned Dougla, an Afro-Indian woman from Trinidad, quite a sight on his arm. Her dark brown hair piled into a bun adorned with golden streaks. She wore understated makeup and light eyeliner around large round eyes. Her symmetrically balanced oval-shaped face, full lips, well-defined cheekbones, delicate nose, round chin and smooth, clear rich honey-colored skin featuring slight brown undertones glowed like a Christmas tree blinding an already overwhelmed Lester.

Abby carried her dual heritage with pride. Lester and Abby smiled, laughed and danced until they ran out of strength. They got along perfectly. Karen was outclassed and already forgotten. No match for Abby, the clear winner; she expressed a strong desire for a harmonious relationship, and a spirit of cooperation and compromise.

She very much wanted to find favor in Lester's eyes, become his gal, the one and only, and to that end was already suppressing meddlesome thoughts of self-doubt and insecurity threatening to keep her from the man she wanted.

Lester regained his mojo, and reopened for business. The African was wrong. Manliness was everything to Lester. He was a man's man. That night, Abby confirmed this much. They went all the way, and then started spending time together every day and became inseparable. The smiling African gladly took back the statement that had so offended Lester. The ploy had worked.

At the rooming house, things were getting weird. The happy-go-lucky taxi driver with a large stash of rubbers brought penniless passengers upstairs to his room for compensation in nature in between fares. When not in class, the cook from the basement, who had no life, no time, no girlfriend, and no visitors, worked in the kitchen of a trendy restaurant.

The visa that brought him to the U.S. precluded him from changing jobs and employers. Should he try, he would risk deportation. Year in year out, without a break, without prospects, under constant pressure he eventually caved psychologically. He started behaving erratically and defecated throughout the house.

He jumped over neighbors' fences, acting out a threatening ritual that guaranteed every time the cops would come to take him away. It happened five times. After each release, if he remembered to take his medication, he remained cool, sedate, and just fine; at least for a while, a tamer version of himself, a zombie really. Most times, however, he forgot to take his magic pills, and eventually lost his mind again, leaving roommates to negotiate stool specimens placed in strategic locations marking an expanding territory. His mind had lost all sense of control over events, and all sense of certainty and possibility. Unhinged, he looked lost in boundless despair. Trying to hold on to a fleeting sense of control over a tenuous existence, neither Lester nor the taxi driver could do much to help the cook.

The morning of the last day Lester spent at the house, there had been a handgun on the kitchen counter. That is all he could see. That black object of death was familiar to Lester. Marilyn's dad had one. He was a cop. Lester remembered him explaining the small military caliber semi-automatic gun was only available for law enforcement. The sight of the perfectly ominous concealed carry firearm stopped Lester in his tracks. He no longer wanted breakfast. The back of the cook still bent over a skillet meant he had not heard him come in. There were no pleasantries to be exchanged that morning. Lester ran back to his room to grab his phone and go as far as he could from the house. Panting, he called the landlord, and explained he could no longer stay in the house. Something had to give. It was either him or the cook.

At that stage he would check into a hotel and wait to get his things when the coast was clear and the cook safely away at work. On second thought, the landlord didn't need to get tangled with the cook. Lester would altogether put an end to his involvement in the drama. At this stage, to continue residing in the same house was unsafe. Even if he left, the deranged man could always come back and exert a bloody revenge should he feel wronged in any way.

After a bad night, no sooner did Lester leave Abby's place, she missed him all over again and blew up his phone. She worried about him. Resenting his absence, she could hardly keep it together; without an appetite she would nibble on food, unable to give her full attention to the task at hand, and prone to sadness, she complained to no end.

"Where were you?" became the question she compulsively asked. She was more fragile than he thought, even prone to panic attacks. After seeing each other for two months, it no longer made sense to maintain a separate place.

Having a partner increased Abby's level of self-confidence while it improved Lester's general well-being and sense of connection. He worried Abby was losing her identity. She had a tendency to become overly dependent on him. Finding the balance between being herself and being his woman was a challenge.

She ached to be with him. There was nothing she wouldn't do to belong to him. And, as she pressed Lester to move into her apartment for good, she wheedled, whined, and pouted until she got what she wanted. Given the circumstances, it made a lot of sense to move in with Abby, except for this little thing called passion that was missing for Lester. There were no butterflies in his belly. To his credit he fancied her and was willing to compromise his heart in the off chance his instinct was right and as he figured, he could trust and believe in her.

True love was overrated. He convinced himself everyone was basically waiting for their turn at that silly game. Abby was a better prospect, an altogether superior woman to Marilyn. Once this point got settled in his mind, he convinced himself of it, he could manage his emotions and decided to go all in! He'd found a home at last.

SUBURBAN BLUES

The boy stopped asking for an allowance; asking his father for money, whether for school or because he truly needed it would trigger an argument. The boy considered his father too cheap; asking felt like pulling teeth. So he carried on instead as if oblivious. Money was no object anymore, at least, he made it seem like it.

As usual, he came and went as he pleased; any sense of deprivation had abandoned him. He acted confident and self-sufficient. That was strange and unsettling to his father! Gerald was a miser who considered his son Mark, lucky. They lived in a nice house in a great neighborhood.

Gerald was a good provider. There was always food in the fridge. He hadn't been as lucky growing up; hadn't always had enough to eat as a child. He remembered people mocking his family because they had been among the poorest of the poor. His single mother supported him and his brother on $13,000 a year. The many deprivations prompted him and his brother to make a pledge that never again they would want for anything and be anyone's laughingstock. Deprivation, he believed, built character. If it'd been good for him, it'd be good for his kids too.

Mark resented that attitude, just like his sister had before him. She'd moved as far away from the man she blamed for making her life a living hell as a teen after the passing of her mother. She died of ovarian cancer and until then had managed to keep a lid on her husband's rough edges. After she was gone, all bets were off. Each person dealt with the sadness the best way they knew how, which involved withdrawing into one's shell where the worst angels of their nature resided.

Unconvinced, Mr. Mclean went looking for anything that could help explain the sudden change in his son's attitude. He no longer felt he had much clout over the boy. While his football game was in full swing on television, he searched the room carefully with enough desperation to keep at it longer than he had planned. Mark's chronic depression went unnoticed and undiagnosed because no one had any compassion or paid real attention to him.

Hopeless and helpless all the time, he was supposed to want for nothing. Home for Mark was with his mother. He missed her more than anything, but acknowledging his pain would force an undesirable introspection. Gerald kept looking and still, he found nothing out of character. Just what you would expect of a normal teenage boy: a few cigarettes stashed away in a drawer, dirty magazines under the bed. It was nothing to warrant a lecture, or justify fussing at the boy in the manner that would satisfy a father's itch.

Gerald Mclean convinced one of his IT buddies to install a tracking device on his son's computer. He couldn't shake the bad feeling he had. His instincts had him believe something stank to high heaven. He could smell foul play but couldn't prove anything. Better safe than sorry, he thought.

While spying on the boy, he uncovered a world of hurt nothing had prepared him for. Retracing his activities online, he found evidence of sexual favors for pay, and multiple indications of drug use.

Northern Virginia had recently become one the top five sex trafficking hubs in the country. The second fastest growing crime targeted suburban boys and girls from broken homes like the Mclean's. Children who suffered from low self-esteem were especially vulnerable; their helicopter parents more often than not unaware their child was involved in the trade. The kids would go to school and be home each night. It was in the hours between school and home that the sex was arranged through Craigslist or some other Internet site.

Barely able to contain the anger that threatened to give him a heart attack, Gerald talked himself down long enough to print out all the evidence he could find. He'd need it to confront Mark. Still frantic, he called his brother, the counselor, for any advice he could glean. Gerald considered locking Mark into a detox center. Whatever it took. No child of his would bring dishonor to the family. As the state comptroller, a scandal of this magnitude would impact his career. What would people say?

He asked about the cost of treatment, all the while cursing the little shit for making his life more miserable. He'd seen his prescription medication disappear at a fast rate and thought nothing of it at the time. He emptied the medicine cabinet, just in case, to make sure he was no longer, if at all, complicit in his son's vices.

Gerald was very afraid and he knew that

whatever was going on, could not be ignored. He'd get to the bottom of it. Something had been amiss for some time. There had been subtle signs. The music Mark listened to had changed for the worse. It was less harmonious, edgier, noise, at best.

Mark didn't bring friends home after school to study or play, nor did he look his old man in the eye. He'd stopped showing interest in girls too, and took to wearing long sleeves in the summer heat. If Gerald couldn't get through to the kid, he'd have a chat with his neighbor, the sheriff, and have him scare Mark a little.

Like he'd done several times this week, the resident sheriff parked his personal vehicle on the side of the senior living facility up the road. Although he was wearing civilian clothing, everyone knew who he was. People were happy he was there. They lived in a very small place, hardly a town. The sheriff went into the building to spend an hour by his ninety-year-old mother's side. For the duration of the visit, she sat in her favorite rocking chair, a gift from another son.

They chatted as if nothing had changed, reminiscing about the good old days. Clark, the sheriff, was happy that his mother was lucid and able to recognize him. Alzheimer's was a tricky condition. Clark never knew what to expect from one day to the next. Feeling the end was near, he came to see his mother as often as he could.

Before taking his leave, Clark went to look for the attending nurse. He wanted to thank her. She'd taken such great care of his mom. The nurse blushed and gave him a hug. It was late. Now, he had to make his way to the station. Duty called. Clark turned the corner, and almost immediately rushed back into the building looking to make a frantic call. His vehicle had been stolen; his county-issued mobile phone and his service revolver were in it as well. In embarrassment, he squatted to the floor, holding his head with both hands. How could a thing like that happen to him?

After they received the news, the police patrolling the county intensified their effort. They focused in on gold colored Toyota Avalons with Virginia plates. The neighboring counties and the state police were alerted. A crown Victoria was dispatched to pick up the sheriff from the senior facility. He had some explaining to do. In the worst case scenario, Clark ran the risk of getting suspended pending an investigation. If any crime was committed with his weapon, he could lose his job. Clark braced himself.

At best, the thief only had a one-hour-advantage over the police if the theft had occurred right after he'd parked his car. It would take more than one hour to reach a big city. Washington, DC, or Richmond, was over two hours away. On open country roads, an alert officer would have little difficulty intercepting the Avalon, unless traffic was heavier than usual, or the thief had switched the car plates.

Statewide a massive effort was under way. Every officer on the prowl wanted to be the one to bring the perp in, and had a service pistol not been involved, they would have considered the whole affair a simple run-of-the-mill investigation. This was different. Someone had to be apprehended as soon as possible before the media got hold of the story. The media would make enforcement look bad. Finding the car and returning the weapon became priority number one.

Helicopters sat at the ready for an order to take off. Several gold colored Toyota Avalons were flashed down on highways around the state. None was the right one. To make matters worse, there was no witness account of the crime. No one could offer a description of the thief. The police were looking for a needle in a haystack. Just outside of Winchester, close to state lines near Maryland and West Virginia, at 5 pm, the gold 2013 Avalon was found abandoned in the parking lot of a strip mall. Half an hour later, a forensic team descended on the vehicle to collect DNA and lift fingerprints.

After taking pictures and confiscating the security tapes from the strip mall, the police impounded the Toyota. The mobile phone was gone, but that was not considered a bad thing, the minute it would get turned on, officers would geo-locate it. The right officer with the right skills would remotely turn it on and then track it. Anything was possible. As for the gun, the feeling was altogether different.

Surveillance cameras revealed a teenager. The kid, as the police started calling him, appeared strung out and disheveled. He walked erratically, creating dread in the faces of the people that passed him by. He must not have been thinking, otherwise, he'd have chosen a less exposed location to dump the car. Unless, of course, he wanted to get caught. Why else target the automobile of a known law enforcement officer?

He needed the attention to showcase his distress. He walked with a limp. He was suffocating, felt constrained, unable to think straight, he wanted to lash out at the injustice of his existence. Enhanced pictures taken from the surveillance cameras eased the process of identifying him. The police looked in databases for clues. They hit the schools and browsed through students' records, and eventually got their big break. They had a name, Mark Mclean. The DNA collected from the butt of a joint left in the officer's car gave the police the confirmation they'd needed.

Not knowing who to turn to, out of desperation, Mark called his sister in California, shortly after the incident, and admitted to her what he'd done, insisting it wasn't his fault.

"I freaked out and lost it. He was going to kill me."

That morning, the police received a call from a man walking his dog. At first they saw it as a distraction from their number one priority. The man reported seeing smoke coming from a house in his neighborhood. A block away from the senior living facility. Crews of firefighters slaved through the day to extinguish the fire.

Investigators descended on the location to search for clues to determine if the fire had been caused by faulty wiring, malice, or was simply the result of an accident. They discovered the charred body of a large man.

The office of the medical examiner later determined he was the father of the subject of the manhunt, and had been shot before the house was set on fire.

All evidence of the crime pointed to his son. Neighbors remembered seeing them argue the previous day. Then later that morning, a woman from California had called to report that her younger brother had admitted to killing their abusive father in self-defense. The address she gave checked out. He'd been erratic on the phone. She suspected he may be depressed and might attempt to take his own life. The police knew they had to hurry and find him.

Within hours of the theft of the Avalon, a person described as a white male in his late teens, about five feet and ten inches tall, slender build, wearing a blue hoodie, jeans, and sunglasses; and his face wrapped in white bandages entered a CVS pharmacy. The kid presented a note demanding prescription narcotics. He patted his waistband to indicate he had a weapon; then made off with a lot of drugs.

Exactly an hour later, in another part of the county, a young man that fit the same description, this time without the bandages passed a bank teller a note demanding money in large and small bills. Again, he indicated he had a gun, which he did not produce. Another hour passed, and on the opposite side of the county, another bank was hit in the same manner.

This time, the young man made off with $11,000. As he exited the building, a dye pack ignited in his pocket ruining some of the money. Investigators eventually identified his fingerprints on the robbery notes, and the bank's surveillance footage clearly showed it was Mark.

Making use of traffic cameras, and a phone tracking system, the police eventually located him. They knew the general vicinity of where he was: an abandoned plant on the neglected part of the largest town in the county, a bleak area long abandoned by families and small mom and pop's shops; dandelion and detritus grew unattended, and the few remaining residents, a mixture of ex-convicts, junkies and unemployed squatters, never bothered to fix broken windows or clean after themselves.

Night and day, a procession of addicts sleepwalked across train tracks and through an open space littered with dead rats and shattered glass from discarded beer and whisky bottles. They moved toward what stood as a former meat processing plant now strewn with used syringes and soiled condoms. There, they found respite, and any drug they needed to soothe their anxiety.

When the police found Mark, it seemed they'd reached him too late. He was lying in the fetal position on a flattened cardboard box, a needle stuck in his forearm. The two officers that discovered him tried to get his attention by slapping him around. He was fast becoming unresponsive, slipping in and out of consciousness.

Recognizing a potential heroin overdose, the officers held his head high and administered a dose of department-issued naxolone through the nose, and then had him airlifted to the closest hospital. Naxolone could quickly reverse the effect of opiates such as heroin, oxycodone, and hydrocodone. They saved Mark's life. He couldn't die, there were too many questions that needed answers.

THE LONGING

At the age of fifteen, David finally free from another's control, started to look for the father he'd never met. His life depended on getting answers to the questions he had. The Internet and social media did not help. It was as if the man was a ghost. Was he ever real? Even Google couldn't find him! He could get nothing out of his mother. On the topic of his father, she remained silent. David never found out why his mother had cut his father from their lives, hoping he would leave her alone and forget them.

When he was a teenager, David wouldn't stop arguing with his mother. Trying to protect the child, she had deprived him of any insight into who his father was. What dark secret was she harboring? He needed to know the truth. Flinching each time in front of her, determined to find out the truth about his origins, a crazed look in his eyes, looking for salvation, his spirit yearning for a flicker of hope, forever disappointed, condemned to absence, ignorance, and oblivion, he'd beat a dead horse in desperation.

What fools called love felt cruel and unforgiving. What unforgivable act was his father guilty of? Why did the son have to pay for the sins of the father? The violence against him, in turn, he inflicted on himself. Reefers, acid and snow numbed the pain of his ignorance. Without a father, an anchor, the woman who had given birth to David had given him a half-life filled with shame, and guilt. It hurt like a death sentence. The four-story building where David's godmother lived looked austere, and overbearing. She lived in all four levels with her husband, an imposing man. Everyone tiptoed around the general. David loved his godmother and she loved him back. As a child, he enjoyed his treks to the bookstore she owned in the capital. She'd have him pick the comics he liked. On birthdays and for Christmas, she'd give him more money than he knew what to do with. When David became a teenager, he knew just what to do with the money. He'd buy more weed, more acid, and more snow.

All he knew for sure was that his father was a Guinean. So, indiscriminate Guineans became his brothers, and none ever offered a useful clue nor the information he needed to satisfy his longing. He'd been lost a long time.

At age 30 everything changed. Africa had changed. By chance, surfing the Internet, David found out about the man's death a week after it'd occurred. When he told his mother, and then his wife, and his boss, the silence grew deafening. No one knew what to say.

They felt nothing, because he felt nothing other than blind sorrow and self-pity. There were no words of comfort for him. It'd taken him twenty years to find the man. Anger caused his eyes to water and his pain to grow. He'd never know him; and he didn't even know if his father cared. He was both free of the burden of longing, and condemned to the absolute, abysmal emptiness of that freedom. There were other names in the notice, those of the wife and the nine children his father had left behind.

For the next ten years, David went on another pursuit, tracking them online to no avail. Many shared the same names. It was like looking for Mr. and Mrs. Smith. You would find them and many more and not know who's who. Some would ask for money for information. They couldn't be the right people.

Once David abandoned all hope, resigning himself to being an oddity, everything changed. A Facebook post shook his world and woke him up to the possibility of a real connection.

It read: "My hands are trembling. I cannot think straight. The picture of who you call your dad, the one you posted, is the picture of my dad. I believe you are my big brother."

Everyone in his friends' list went on overdrive, teasing and commenting on the weird happening. One unexpected message from a stranger led to an avalanche of heartfelt expressions of sympathy. His life became a skit for all to watch. Happy beyond words, he would get to know the nine brothers and sisters left behind. From that time on, he was on the phone every day, he lived and breathed Guinea.

He remembered all the names, the official and unofficial ones. He had to learn them all; eighteen nieces and nephews too. He received a crash course in family history; found out more than he could process. He finally belonged somewhere; and had become the new father figure. He looked just like him. At long last, he was part of something bigger than himself.

Two of his six new sisters called every single day as if to make up for lost time. Sometimes for no other reason than to hear his voice, say hello, and cry!

A month went by in a blink. He'd become less edgy, more grounded, his loneliness now compromised. Letting go of the silence he'd grown accustomed to, felt uncomfortable. They were his sisters, beautiful and real. He'd never had any sisters!

One Sunday, pretty Claudine woke him up. This had never happened the whole time they'd been siblings, in the four weeks they'd known each other online. It was five in the morning. Could she not understand how precious sleep was when nothing compelled an early rise? David's groggy voice prompted a quick apology, and a promise she would call back a couple of hours later.

Three hours had already passed when Claudine called back. She went straight to the heart of the matter and demanded money, ten thousand dollars, no less, to start a small business, she said. David's words became scarce, his breathing stopped. A great sadness came over him. What a shame!

He had never met Claudine and had only a month ago become aware of her existence; he knew nothing of the life she led. Now she wanted money wired from across the ocean. Thoughts of disowning her percolated in his brain. What a sobering introduction to one of his African sisters!

He was disappointed. He wanted so much to believe she was different from the clichés. Claudine's morality became Africa's morality. An unfair foregone conclusion motivated by bias. Would David still plan to go and meet after that? Would he allow Claudine or anyone else to break his longing heart, broken so many times before? That day though, she made him feel like a king. She thought he was the one that could.

Maybe because of his mother. Stuck in an unresolved past, David longed for the absent. He ran from commitment whenever it beckoned. He'd had a streak of unlucky relationships one after the other. Given a choice, he'd gone for the comfort of connection rather than a more exclusive arrangement.

Emotionally, he'd been unavailable. Insecure, worried he would get dumped, he'd been dumped before, so now at a mere sign of trouble, anticipating the worst, he did the dumping himself. For a year, he'd carried in his wildest dreams an impossible connection. She'd been his girlfriend, had known him well, and was clear as to what she'd be getting into should she agree to revisit the past. Hurt by his dalliance, she'd wanted nothing to do with him.

He was damaged goods; a slave to a powerful dysfunction. They almost didn't get married.

Back then David slept in International House, a three-floor-co-ed building that served as a home to a select group of foreign students, visiting foreign professors, and a few natives interested in foreign languages and international studies. The idyllic location had a bucolic feel; nestled in a historic town of 5,000; surrounded by green pastures, the college campus sat on 112 acres.

The only two recent arrivals among the visiting researchers, they'd been tap-dancing around each other all semester. So a friendship could develop, Yang at long last approached David, and they started to chat. She invited him to join her group in the cafeteria, and introduced him to her friends, an odd assortment of women from every continent; a bi-racial woman from Namibia, two sisters from Sri Lanka, a girl from Panama, another from Thailand, a Spaniard and a Brit, as different from each other in taste, style, and sensibility.

As if to make up for a slow start, in a few days, David showed more interest in Yang than most people had in her short year in the U.S.

Her English was impeccable. He was amazed to learn that as Chinese as she was, she considered herself a Muslim; one of 23 million in China. She gave David an earful, open to satisfying his flattering curiosity.

"Two percent of the Chinese population call themselves Sunni Muslims, that represents ten ethnic groups throughout China. You know, some Chinese people are also Jewish."

"How come I never knew any of this?" David wondered.

"They practice their faith in secret." Weirdest of all, Yang did not believe in God. She professed no religious views and was a Muslim only in name and heritage. She claimed her group had been much less oppressed than the Uyghur. Her ethnic Hui people, lacking separatist sentiments, had been complicit in helping put down Uyghur rebellions. Because of their likeness to the dominant Han, they'd enjoyed greater religious freedom than the Turkic Uyghur who endured state sanctioned oppression and violence.

"The Hui," she said, are linguistically and ethnically similar to the Han with the exception that they practice Islam. We are basically Hans who have converted. We're considered the good Muslims in China."

The more she talked, the more David's new

friend fascinated him. Eager for more, he did some research on his own. Yang had been correct in saying the Han and the Hui were virtually indistinguishable, yet it was also true that their blood carried traces of Persian, Central Asian, and Arab DNA.

Yang was growing on David in a way he could not control. She titillated his intellect. The more lively she became, the more he listened, and the more beautiful she looked, with her lips pursed, fragrant skin, long flowing black hair, symmetrical features, delicate face, and subtle manners.

On weekends, they strolled through winding tree-lined red-brick sidewalks on their way to the waterfront where a boat awaited; then paddled aimlessly for hours. The ritual served as an excuse to spend time in each other's company. On a quest to appropriate each other's worlds, they chatted non-stop and on occasions exchanged an awkward touch.

Looking at him softly one day, in a brazen show of affection, Yang placed a warm hand on David's arm. He needed not be so timid with her. Frazzled, he understood she fancied him too. The small gesture freed him of his self-consciousness. From the witty sense of humor to the round and tiny mouth and the clear bright almond-shaped eyes, David enjoyed everything about Yang. She could lose herself in the intensity of his lust. Free to transform away from home, Yang dived into the eddies of her flailing libido, experiencing, yet dismissing the pull of her ancestral culture warning against it. She ached for David and lacked the strength to take heed. There was no taming his love either. They would only be whole when the flesh met the flesh and their desires collided.

Yet, a long kiss is all she would concede for now, as the world, as she'd always known it, was shattering around her. She'd taken for granted that she could never fall for a darker person. They spent the night huddled on a single bed wrestling with desire, then knocked down by fatigue, they slept tumescent and sore. Yang wanted to sound out the depth of his devotion before surrendering her virginity and throwing caution to the wind. She needed to know he'd be there to catch her if she fell. She felt strong and almost ready. David refrained, decided to wait, wanting her to surrender without prompt or regret; in her own time.

The next morning, on the way to class, Yang reached for and grabbed his warm, reassuring hand. They walked hand in hand, then happened upon a small group they both knew. In a sudden and cowardly attempt to look cool, David let go of Yang's hand in a most cavalier manner, and triggered in her a rush of sadness. She clammed up, moved by the realization that he had not shared her commitment, nor understood how portent the moment had been. He was like that David, indecisive, and fickle.

Between them suddenly words became meaningless. The gesture had been clear, painful and swift. It brought back memories of pain, of the unbreachable distance between them. They were not one as she had thought, but two distinct human beings, torn, thrown into a bottomless gulf. Within a week Yang had disappeared. She left campus without saying a word to anyone. No one knew where she was. It was then that David fully appreciated how he'd hurt her. He'd noticed the way she froze in the instant of his betrayal but had not taken the full measure of his action even though a few seconds after she'd ran the other way.

Stepping out of a subway wagon a year later in Washington, D.C., David noticed a familiar silhouette brushing past him in an effort to climb into the train. On the platform he turned around and squinted to make sure he took in the view. Attired in a dark business suit, Yang, feeling the weight of someone's gaze, looked up as the wagon door was closing. The train started moving as David raised a hand to his ear as if holding a phone. She understood what he meant, and quickly mouthed off without a single sound:

"Call me!"

Was he not allowed a moment of self-doubt, as visible as his had been? "Why had I been so quick to write him off because of it?" she thought to herself. There was much she wanted to apologize for. She would look him up. During the time of their separation, David had convinced himself that Yang had returned to China. Maybe that is exactly what she had wanted him to believe. She was once again within reach, and he would track her down.

She'd clearly been moved when she noticed him; and had even reached for the door to join him on the platform. That was all David needed to know, that anything was still possible. That could well be the break he needed to get over his failing. He had to find Yang and make amends. With some effort, within the week he found her number. She agreed to have dinner. A big fan of Ping Pong Dim Sum, an Asian fusion restaurant in Chinatown, Yang took David to the place she enjoyed the most for its relaxing décor and chic atmosphere. Between them, they ordered seven dishes, which was plenty for two people. By the end of the evening, he knew his dream of resuming where they'd left off was fast becoming a reality; they were drinking wine from each other's cup, and wanting him to taste her favorite food, Yang guided her chop sticks to his eager palate.

Daydreaming, she said:

"And to think I almost lost you, the man of my dreams. For what? Because I felt you did not meet one of my unrealistic romantic expectations of consistency, one time? I feel so shallow."

"That, you're not. Life is messy. Together, we'll deal with it."

"David, we have to get this thing right. I don't want us to fail."

He just knew it. All would be well.

The first time he'd tried, full of hang-ups and fretful, the wedding had to be postponed. His nerves wouldn't let him go through with it. Afraid and still insecure, he did not truly believe himself worthy of love. He'd grown up fearing abandonment, but this time, he had to press on and go through with it. He wouldn't get another chance to redeem himself.

After all, it was not just anybody, but Yang he was marrying, the only woman he'd ever loved. He'd already committed to do it, and she accepted the ring. Each time though, the very thought of marriage triggered anxiety. Overthinking could only spell his doom. She now knew of his affliction and proved patient. He would honor the decision they'd made.

The wrong look, the wrong word, the wrong gesture had the power to unravel the relationship. He was on probation, walking a tight rope.

After the wedding, jealousy, and control, he worried, might destroy all autonomy. David had to get a grip over his thoughts. He felt at home with Yang. For the man she loved, she'd sacrificed friends and family, none of whom understood her choice. She needed him unafraid and as determined as she was. Her belly was showing. They were expecting.

The day they appeared at the Justice of the Peace, couples in line ahead of them with their bouncy party took pity on David and his very pregnant bride. There were no witnesses to their union; no friends or family on either side. Their sight dimmed the light on what was to be a joyous occasion; as if a wet blanket had been cast on the anticipation of merrymaking.

Eager to drive out the distraction, the couples in wait graciously and in unanimity elected to let David and Yang go first. There are many Davids dancing in scorned theaters of despair all because of missing childhood memories; some stuck, others like him getting unstuck through the miraculous power of love. Who knows what would have become of them, had they had different memories?

THE WIND BENEATH

"You will never amount to anything. You've ruined my life. I regret the day you came into this world." Jen lashed out and took her anger out on her son whenever something went wrong. This time, she'd failed to obtain the job she wanted. Had she gotten it, she was convinced life would have been sweeter. She would have it made. Working in the school cafeteria would mean benefits and health insurance and she needed all of it. The pay would have been enough to move out of her mother's basement once and for all. Jen pined for a little distance between her and that damn despair that just wouldn't let go.

She felt useless, utterly, and whenever fate reminded her how much of a loser she was, she'd punish the child; he was after all the most concrete evidence of her failings.

Still a young 28-year-old attractive blonde with a perfect figure, she caused a stir when she walked down the street. Women resented her for it while men turned around so they could catch another glimpse of her. Jennifer enjoyed the catcalls. She craved the attention. It made her wish for a life without Jim. He was the reason why she still wasn't happy and didn't have it good. "Take him away. I don't want this kid. I just can't stand him. I don't want him to call me mommy anymore!"

Jen pleaded with a concerned social worker. Mrs. Rockwell, who at that precise moment wished the boy had not been within earshot, and deplored the mother's rant; he heard everything. Jim always was around, close by, whenever his mother hit the ceiling. It was not the first time she had said these things in front of him. And she was the only person that took care of him, fed him the peanut butter and jelly sandwiches he loved to eat.

She gave him milk. He called her mommy. That's all he ever knew. When he was a nice boy, and she felt good, she patted him on the head, making him feel loved. This was the closest he'd ever been to joy. He was six.

Mrs. Holloway, Jen's mother, and Jim's grandmother, watched the outburst as usual. She took a slow drag from her cigarette, and shook her head as she sat near the living room window in her favorite armchair. A big stain, coffee, maybe, made it look cheap. It was worn out and bleached by the sunlight. She could afford neither a replacement nor a good ole steam-cleaning. Her daughter's misgivings about being the boy's mother and rejection of him was a scene she'd seen repeated many times before. In her family, it was a rite of passage.

Her entire life, that's how parents treated their kids. Typically, she'd intervene and put an early end to the madness, but Mrs. Holloway didn't say a word. It wasn't the right time, and she did not wish to add to the confusion by raising her voice. There was company. Jen would eventually get a grip, calm down, and everything would be normal again. She would accept her fate like everyone else, until the next time Hell broke loose.

Tired of having neighbors calling her to that house, Mrs. Rockwell resolved to make a determination. She had enough of the family. She was prepared to do what she thought was right for the boy once and for all. Was it or was it not in his best interest to remain with the only family he had ever known? A separation would be brutal. Good or bad, for six years the two women had been his kin. Sure, they showed little to no kindness, but life was hard in these parts.

The thought of leaving the boy put, open to his mother's abuse, tugged at the social worker. What would people say? That she'd lost her touch. She didn't care anymore. She would argue it was just another case, but if anything serious happened to the boy, everyone would say it was her fault, she'd failed to take action when she'd had the chance.

And that terrible mother, Jen, wasn't making her job any easier, going around, telling every soul she knew, she didn't want to be anybody's momma; and how that demon child was ruining her life. What a bothersome family!

The Holloway mother and daughter team bickered all the time. When the social worker asked them separately to describe the atmosphere at home, "toxic" is the word each used. No one ever left. They needed each other. Seven years prior, after an evening of drunkenness at a local bar where Jen allowed men to buy her liquor, she ended up in a motel with a young man she'd never met. He'd caught her fancy. She'd never see him again.

He talked funny, in long sentences and all, with an accent; not the grunts she was accustomed to. She didn't bother with his name, and he didn't bother with hers. It didn't matter. Strangers' names never do! Two months later upon finding out she was pregnant, she considered an abortion. Her mother's mind was made up. Nothing Jen said made a difference. She was to keep the child, her mother insisted, and it was final. They were good Christian folk.

Jim was a social boy with lots of friends in the neighborhood. They would let him be the hero in their games. Their favorite was hide and seek: he was a cape-wearing justice seeker, an avenger tracking miscreants and protecting the community.

They played for hours, until the adults inevitably came to crash the party and send his posse home. When not on punishment at school, the teachers described Jim as one of the smartest boys in the class. A real pleasure to teach. Lately, he'd been home, barred from school due to antisocial behavior; he overheard an adult say, not knowing what that meant. The social worker soon found out, that advocating on his behalf felt like a waste of time.

No one liked the boy; not the parents, nor the teachers. He didn't fit in. He carried the mark of infamy, some thought. The principal wouldn't give an inch. Jim, she said, did not get along with anyone unless he was in charge. His displays of aggression made him a liability to the establishment. Jim had told a classmate he was too stupid to be allowed to live, and had raised his voice at the teacher who disciplined him for it, telling her she was a good for nothing moron.

Other parents had been complaining. Always the first to clown around and the first to fly off the handle, he was keeping their children from learning and focusing in class. He had too many emotional problems, and didn't belong in a mainstreamed classroom. Other arrangements had to be made. Other than referring the boy to an appropriate establishment, there was nothing further the school could do for him.

A short while afterward Mrs. Rockwell, the social worker, took Jim from the only home he'd ever known. She managed to have him placed temporarily in a foster home. The family that received him already had four foster boys. The house mother, a pious and kind matron saw it as her duty to bring some measure of humanity to the lives of the wayward souls under her care. She would be their shepherd.

She taught them to join hands in prayer, to care for one another like brothers in Christ, and earn their keep by helping around the house. She tried her hardest to connect with Jim. Having received so little in his short life, he was resistant to human touch and affection. It wasn't easy! He recoiled every time she approached.

Her husband, the disciplinarian, had a much easier time getting through to Jim. He laid down the law with a no-nonsense attitude. Jim understood verbal abuse and violence; being on the other side of love was nothing new. It was familiar and predictable. So the injunctions of the burly man did not faze him. He would get no trouble out of Jim.

Jen reached out to the social worker. She needed to find out how her son was doing, and what type of people were taking care of him. Shaking while she spoke; looking desperate for answers, she added:

"A nice professional family would be perfect. They'd provide for Jim, and who knows, maybe agree to extend some assistance to his folks as well?"

Exasperated by what she saw as erratic behavior, Mrs. Rockwell, in the nicest voice she could manage, answered her questions and then asked her not to worry about Jim anymore. She'd given him up after all, and staying connected to a child she rejected would only confuse him.

"I did not give him up. I just could not take care of him. It's complicated. You know? There's a difference." She said.

While in church, in the second row of neatly lined pews, Jim and his foster brothers sat sheepishly in prayer; just the way the family wanted it. Trying not to draw attention to himself, he mimicked the rehearsed gestures of the adults around him. He bent his knees, lowered his head and took a contrite, pensive air of deep contemplation. Jim put his hands together to his foster mother's delight. He could be such a good boy.

The sermon that day stressed the need to repent of one's sins in order to find favor with God. Jim racked his brain looking for a sin he might have committed. His new mother had explained what a sin was; it was doing something you knew you shouldn't do. He could think of nothing. His memory at that age was shallow, much like his understanding of the whims of adults.

He then looked at his foster father lost in deep conversation with a person he couldn't see, up in the ceiling, eyes looking up and palms raised high above his head imploring an invisible force. The intensity of the man's devotion awed Jim. His facial muscles twitched keeping the boy's eyes riveted.

A woman dressed in black sat in the back of the church on the farthest seat from the center aisle. She wore a light veil like one of the devout old ladies in the front. Ignoring the tears streaking down her face, she watched the burly man with his hands up in the air and the little boy quizzically observing him. She appeared in the rear two Sundays in a row. Jim looked well, neither sad nor happy, each time he mostly seemed confused. Jen thought it best to stay away for good. She'd done everything she could do for him.

After a long day dutifully following directions, weary and no longer able to focus after two hours of a long sermon, Jim grew antsy and started tapping a foot. The frown on his face signaled how bored he was. These signs of impatience inevitably would surely be misconstrued as further evidence of his unruly nature.

A lack of faith and devotion to the word of Almighty God had to be severely punished. And while we were at it, why not also chastise Jim for wetting his bed night after night? His lack of self-control was both an affront and an imposition on the household. Someone had to clean up his mess.

Jim's foster father would give him the paddle and make him an example to the other children. The paddle would not leave marks. That'd be ungodly! The father always aimed at the buttock. Quite a naturally layered part of the human anatomy. It was most padded with clothing after church. He saw it as stamping out evil, making the world a better place where the Devil could find no solace. The first time he was hit, Jim cowered in disbelief and hurt. Sleep would not find him. He spent the night shriveled up and awake in the corner of his bed.

He wondered why fate had been so unkind to him, why he was born evil and unlovable. Other kids had people who loved and treated them nicely. No wonder they could afford to be kind! He decided that night that if people thought him so evil, he'd have to live out his destiny, be evil, and hurt in turn those who hurt him. The last time it happened, the third time in four weeks he'd received a thrashing after he'd been placed in the Christian home, from his pocket he pulled out a match stolen from the kitchen and, in a daze, full of a fury brought about by distress, he used it to set his bed ablaze. He wanted to destroy his place in that wicked house.

A Bible in one hand, the nice old couple, voguing in highly stylized humble poses and meek faces, a knowing smile at the ready, not daring to look Jim's way, explained to the government people that came to get him back why they no longer desired to keep the troubled child. Mrs. Rockwell seemed at a loss. There was no room at the orphanage. If one was to believe all that had been said about him, Jim was clearly deranged. For one, he was incapable of empathy. She could see his blank stares. He didn't appreciate how he made everybody's life a living Hell. Why couldn't he just behave? She would have him evaluated and probably interned after the summer, once space became available.

Passed out on a hotel bed too big for his small frame, a smug grin on his face, Jim seemed happy at last. The night nurse looking over him attempted, carefully, to tuck him in, she tried not to wake him—. She knew too well how he disliked being touched. Her replacement would be there at eight in the morning.

When you first meet the boy, he acts much like a little adult with a real sense of purpose, she thought, the likes of which she'd never seen in a little package.

His self-importance might have been a vain attempt to protect a bruised ego. The nurse could not forget even for a minute what the boy had done. She had to remain alert. All it would take for the worst to happen is an instant. She could not afford to fall asleep in his presence. That could cost her the job.

She pulled out a book from her bag, glanced at the child snoring lightly, passed out onto the large bed, and when she reckoned that all was well, the coast was clear, she started browsing. She opened the book where she had left off the night before, wondering how a six-year-old boy could end up all alone in the world in a hotel room paid for by taxpayers, as a ward of the state, instead of with a foster family, in an orphanage, or with his family on the other side of town.

All she'd been told was that he'd tried to kill people. That angelic face, easy smile, and affectionate ways made the quick-witted kid a pleasure to work with. How could that be? Sure, on occasions he had to be disciplined, but no more and no less than a regular kid. Once she got to know Jim, she concluded he was really no trouble at all. How could the supervisor be right? What really happened? She would ask again, and this time also request to see the child's file when she went to the office. What she would find would probably tear her heart to shreds and bring her to tears, but she needed to know. She'd become obsessed with Jim!

The boy's mother had been abused by her mother, who had also been abused by her mother. They were all abuse survivors. None of the people in that family had finished high school. Few had ever held a job. Men stuck around long enough to sire the next child. The family survived on a welfare check from the government and handouts from the church and other charitable organizations. The disability check Jim's grandmother was also getting made all the difference and paid for amenities like the cable and other distractions.

The beds of flowers in the park, tulips, roses, and lilies, and the lawn that surrounded them remained off limits to passers-by and strollers. An oasis in the middle of a concrete jungle, the park attracted all manner of nannies and mothers accompanied by young children. Office workers sometimes stood by at the edge of the green while taking a break to draw on a cigarette, polluting the air. To avoid being forced to move, vagrants sat up at the first sighting of a police officer. Happy children ran around playing tag and laughing boisterously. He loved balls. If there was a ball of any sort,

Jim joined in the fun. When he lost himself in the activity, the world smiled.

Otherwise, he did the unthinkable. Under the watchful but permissive eye of the attending nurse, the one that took him to the park in the morning, he picked forbidden flowers. His love of flowers could simply not be argued with. Like him, they were plucked from their roots, added pizzazz to people's lives, gave of themselves while no longer receiving their sustenance. Jim made a colorful assortment.

Upon returning to the hotel, he looked for Ada, his favorite attendant, and offered her the bouquet with his brightest smile. He had a thing for Ada. She liked him back, and left a slice of cake in the room the day after. Jim told a nurse how he wished Ada could stay with him all the time.

"The nurse," she insisted, "is a bad influence on my child."

When pressed to explain what she meant, Jen hesitated, then blurted:

"She allows him to disregard the rules and pick up flowers from the park. There are signs, you know, that clearly forbid it."

Mrs. Rockwell repressed the urge to smack her. Instead, she answered in a calm voice.

"We've been through this already. Please, stay away from the child, or I'll have no choice but to involve the judge."

She came to tidy up, vacuum the room, make the bed, and clean the bathroom, and Jim sometimes refused to leave. He'd sit down in a deep, cushy chair and watch her move about with the grace of a feline. She smiled at him often, and he smiled back, mesmerized with her soft gaze and gentle ways. No one had ever been as kind to him as Ada before. She tiptoed around his pain. Concerned, she saw the scared little boy for what he was, hungry for acceptance, and some measure of love.

"Why can't you be my mummy?" he once asked.

To Jim, she was more than a mortal; she was a guardian angel. Happy, in her presence, he came alive. Warmth enveloped him as if for the first time, and blood rushed through his veins. He felt loved.

Ada Bakary loved receiving flowers from Jim. In conversations with colleagues, she referred to him as her littlest man. The hotel staff, for the most part, a group of West

Africans, were fond of Jim. He gave them no trouble, only joy, and showed great curiosity.

The pain that had been visited upon the mixed child had come from his own people, a little paler than him. He looked like an Arab. With the Blacks, his anger died. They did not seem to expect the worst from him. There was complicity, as if they understood his pain. They took pity on him. The nurses' supervisor was well aware that there had been fewer incidents when black nurses, male or female, attended to the child; so she encouraged the practice.

The morning nurse recorded in Jim's file, as a significant event, the day Ada first received the flowers. Jim looked at home with Ada, and had shown empathy and not bolted when, moved to tears, she had placed a friendly hand on his shoulder. She'd wanted him to know how much his kind gesture had meant to her. Her own husband never thought to bring her flowers, not even on her birthday. No adult had ever been able to touch Jim without causing a meltdown, not the nurses that cared for him, not the teachers at his previous school, and when she came to visit once a month, not even the woman he no longer called mom. He'd made up his mind, just like she'd made up her mind. His real mom was now Ada.

THE UNRAVELING

1

As usual, my early-morning routine is hectic. I am once again leaving my small apartment without eating breakfast. No time. I wish I could avoid speeding on the beltway to arrive on campus in time for the class I am supposed to teach at eight. I have no clue how long I can avoid getting a speeding ticket.

Pacing the floor of the university classroom outside of Baltimore, making eye contact with no one, on the morning of September 11, 2001, I am well into a lecture when an alarmed student rushes to the front of the class, and without asking permission, turns on the television set mounted on the wall. The images of people jumping out of windows to their deaths are jarring. The stillness of my transfixed body clashes with the spontaneous chaos and the cacophony of ring tones and screams that suddenly erupt. Within seconds, students are rushing out the door. I feel like I am having déjà vu. My keen sense of purposelessness evaporates. At that moment, in outrage, I vow to join the fight against terrorism. There is no better way to regain a sense of control and to restore certainty in my life. I pledge to bring all of my talents to bear for this newfound purpose.

I am bored. Helping privileged, talented, and driven students offers no intellectual stimulation. Competitive as they are, they do not need me to make their way in their lives. Even a bad teacher could not stop them from achieving good grades. My restless mind thrives on high-minded projects. I need to feel that I am making a difference. I ache for the natural high that feeling gives me. I cannot wait to be totally engrossed in activities that are fun and rewarding. I enjoy autonomy and strive for the freedom to choose how I channel my energy. I desire power, that ability to make things happen and long for status and quiet recognition for a job well done. I am needy.

Early this evening the phone rings. It is Sherawonda.

"Good evening, sir. Shera speaking."

Not long ago, she had been a student in my class; since then, she had become a successful lawyer. As a teen, before joining the university, her mother's crack addiction landed them in a homeless shelter. She badly wanted out of that life. Never complaining, always prepared for class, she applied herself and made it a point to shine. I saw myself in her; trusted and believed in her abilities. People like her are the reason I became a teacher. I believe in the transformative power of education.

"Hello, Sherawonda. Nice to hear your voice again." She was one of the very best I had ever taught. Writing her a recommendation for law school had been an honor.

"Am I calling at a bad time? Can we talk?"

"Absolutely. Now is a fine time to talk."

"Did you think about what we discussed last time? My brother thinks—"

"Oh yeah. Well, I will take him up on his offer this time. I just need to clear my head and figure out how to proceed."

"Oh, great news. Remember, I know you will be happier doing something that matters to more people. Gotta talk to him. May I give him your number?"

"Yes, no problem. But let's not get ahead

of ourselves here. I dunno if—"

"Don't worry, sir. Everything will be okay. Take care for now. I need to call him."

Sherawonda wanted to help her brother, a recruiter for a governmental agency. He had told her about how difficult it was to find good language instructors capable of securing a clearance.

The Office of Recruitment called me twice before I finally got around to submitting an application. One year later, in October 2002, during the twenty-three days of fear that the Washington, DC snipers inflicted on the region, I venture out to submit myself to a series of interviews and tests. Each time, I rush back home to avoid being shot. The last thing I want is to become another casualty on the evening news. The shooting spree in the DC metro area culminated with ten people killed and three others critically injured.

Fear is nothing new to me. She is an old pal. I have felt powerless before; terrorist attacks had plagued and interrupted my childhood. Bombs left in street bins, on subway platforms, in shopping areas, in restaurants, and in police stations had unsettled and destroyed all expectations of peace and stability. Pro-independence separatists, right-

and left-wing extremists, pro-Palestinian freedom fighters used to run rampant while I was growing up.

The government agency's test in my native French is the hardest I have ever taken. Two elderly women are drilling me machine-gun-style, intent on tripping me up. I am French, by way of the islands; I was born in Guadeloupe and taken to France at the age of two. Throughout my youth, I have flown back and forth between the French West Indies and Europe every two to three years.

In the writing section of the test, I answer a series of random questions. Next, the psychological assessment. It is long and uninspiring—like all psychological assessments. The psychologist, a pale, old, disheveled weirdo refuses to shake hands. He has a large coffee stain on his white shirt. The weirdo provides some levity. He looks more in need than most of the services he offers. Finally, a polygrapher asks about my sex life, fun, fun (does he need tips?); the number of women I have been with, how I spend my money, the type of friends I keep, and my alcohol and drug use. His tone makes the session long and dreary. On two occasions, I even fall asleep. Boring! Otherwise, unnerved, wanting to spice things up, stay awake and have some fun, I reveal that I had been a pothead in my teenage years. The man does not flinch. In the end, I leave the room drained and annoyed for subjecting myself to this. I no longer care whether I get the job.

I convince myself Sherawonda's brother has made me the butt of a sick joke. He has told me that the government desperately needs people who speak foreign languages. I am fluent in three of them. Could it be that my dual citizenship is the problem? I shrug off the whole thing as a bad trip. All hopes of ever hearing back from the recruiter are gone.

An eternity goes by. Two months before the second summer after the polygraph, I receive an official offer in the mail. A huge sense of relief, mixed with resentment, comes over me. What a rollercoaster! I give up my annual summer vacation and start working for the government in mid-July 2003. Almost two long years have elapsed between the time I had applied for the position and what is to be my first day on the job. This must be some job!

2

It is five in the morning. I open my eyes slowly. They seem glued. The ringtone irks me. I want to throw the damn clock against the wall. Why am I waking up earlier than usual? I stretch and take my time before getting out of bed, just as I normally do. This time, I am not alone. I am not a morning person. I shower slowly, and then hurry to get on the beltway.

Last night, I had a conversation with Barbara, my girlfriend. She is the perfect woman—a wild cougar. I am thirty, she is fifty. We met two years ago outside of Baltimore on the university campus where she is the dean. Her firm, perky body, protruding backside, dignified deportment, sexy brown skin, high cheekbones, and impeccable attire, drew my attention immediately.

My name is Antoine. I am a dog. A French poodle, she insists. I want a break from the relationship and lament the difference in our ages—After all, the gap is wide. What will my mother think? Furthermore, I will soon be moving to Virginia, away from Maryland and starting a new life in which there is no room for distractions. For sure, Barbara was a great help. She trained me well and gave me my mojo back.

Now, I have this need to take stock of my life, do something else, explore the inner workings of my soul.

Leaning forward, she squints, listens intently, dispassionately, it seems. Then asks lots of questions, all sorts, and keeps her thoughts private. I am sweating. The woman knows how to put the fear of God in my heart.

This morning, when I awake, she smiles broadly before she says to me, "On this special day, you can't rush out on an empty stomach. No sir. It's not happening. I have made you a big breakfast. Let's eat in bed, honey." She is so kind. Big relief. She never ceases to amaze me. Such grace and understanding! Everything will be alright after all. Phew!

In moderate traffic, it takes me over two hours to reach the office. Staring at the cloudless sky, I cannot help but think how wonderful my life is shaping up to be. Head held high, filled with a sense of purpose, I sing all the way. I am happy and proud.

It is my first day on the job. Could it be the excitement? I am not certain of what has caused the indigestion. The internal movements of my bowels are excruciating. My smiles looked more like grimaces that day. I spent more time than I cared for sitting on a commode and became well acquainted with the men's room on the office floor that day.

The language school feels like a mini–United Nations with twenty-five languages represented, but one whose mission is to equip employees with the cultural know-how and linguistic agility to advance American interests around the world. A sea of repetitive and regimented six-foot-tall cubicles crowds a huge space crisscrossed by narrow lanes. Each cluster accommodates a language group.

To be of any utility, language trainers keep abreast of the latest international developments; relearn their national histories; and plug into the cultural trends, ways of thinking, and perspectives popular in their countries of origin. About fifty trainers provide training on demand, both on a one-on-one basis and in small groups of five, five hours a day, five days a week, year-round. Every day for up to two hours, they conduct language-proficiency tests and spend the rest of the day in course preparation, translations, or interpretations, as assigned.

Teaching literature is out of the question. It distracts from government business. War terminology is what students want. At the drop of a hat, they have to be able to employ foreign language skills and charm to weigh in on discussions with foreign counterparts. Without these, training is a disaster. Each trainer exhibits the stereotypes that his or her cultural group is known for. They embody to perfection the American expectations of their ethnicities and national origins. Maintaining that foreignness proves most profitable. In times of crises, trainers turn into regional consultants with insight into other cultures.

Naturalized U.S. citizens for the most part, the trainers take great care to not bewilder the natives. U.S.-born employees tolerate the foreign-born. Less comfortable with the English language, the older generation has learned to not draw attention to itself. A yahoo may take exception to their inclusion. The tyranny of the native language, which earns them their daily bread, slows their integration into the larger workforce and their mastery of difficult linguistic concepts in English.

The training rooms are some ways away from the trainers' vault and separated by a long hallway and massive doors. Visitors have to be buzzed into the vault. Cameras are hidden in both the training and the testing rooms. Phone and computer usage are strictly monitored, and all keystrokes are logged. We are always on. It is exhausting!

3

Before she retires, an elderly French instructor whom I enjoy talking to convinces me that real life events generate more interest in students. Authentic materials must be systematically included in lessons from the get-go. She explains how she helped a middle-aged student learn French. Outside the classroom, she expected him to complete three hours of study on his own. For class, she picked what she believed to be an excellent textbook, full of drawings and simple, easy-to-understand explanations, yet failed to connect with him. The student was not learning as fast as others in the class. Most of the time, he seemed bored and impatient with the material. She wondered whether that was due to a lack of motivation and reckoned that if a student was not paying attention, he was not going to change and improve. Then one day, just for fun, she brought a newspaper article to class, and everything changed. The reticent student grew eager to decipher a story that he knew was relevant to his life. He started working diligently with a dictionary and a grammar book and asked lots of questions. All the while, the instructor could not help but worry she was losing control of the instruction. The student then launched into a labored yet meaningful conversation about the article. The experience provided the opening she had sought. Her frown transformed into the broadest smile.

Back in the classroom, I took the story to heart and made the use of stimulating, authentic materials a staple of my instruction, and kept students working on activities they found meaningful. The success I experienced prompted Lea, a manager, to handpick me to present at a language conference. My topic: the use of authentic materials to engage students and promote better learning. The manager wants to see a draft of the presentation. She edits and reorganizes my thoughts, neglecting to inquire as to what prompted them. Every step of the way, she orders me to change a word here, punctuation there, a picture in a slide, the color, and the font... I comply; show her the changes she requests on ten different occasions. Whenever she belches, I am expected to jump. Each one of her brain farts becomes a dictate. The unending dance back and forth quickly stops making sense. The day before the presentation, annoyed, I decide against showing her the final change of font. After all, I am the one who is going to be speaking from the notes. What does she care what it looks like?

I start right on time, to address a packed conference hall. People are leaning against the walls and sitting on the floor. There must be at least three hundred of them. The audience is wildly responsive: only one person leaves during the presentation. I remember him. I had turned down the badly paid, part-time position he had offered me at his Baltimore establishment.

In stumbles the director of the language school the minute I lose that sucker. She looks pissed. Blocking the line of sight of dozens of attendees, she stands across from me and stands there rigidly, legs far apart samurai-style with arms crossed. Resisting the urge to cower, I keep going without breaking a sweat. The curmudgeon squints, takes aim, and launches darts at me with her eyes. She despises anyone who challenges authority. An hour later, I complete the presentation to raucous applause. Before the noise subsides, in a huff, the director exits the hall. Despite the many people who request my contact information and an opportunity to chat, I know I have lost favor with my school by asserting my independence over the font I used.

Fair-skinned,   fine-featured,   petite,

Nordic-looking, a miniature version of Uma Thurman, Leila is a good teacher. In me, she triggers smiles of subdued joy whenever I see her. Working together is a hoot. We started at the language school on the same day. We eat together, laugh at the same jokes, help each other, share tips on how to do the job better, cover for each other, and are seen together so much people are starting to gossip. More than most, Leila is high on life. Although comfortable only with those she already knows and usually awkward in social situations, she makes friends with the few kind, down-to-earth black people she meets in the building. Enough to add to the rumors. Scandalmongers are of a mind that her affinity for black people is only about one thing, sex. The cynics just cannot understand it.

It did not take long. Despite the good company I keep, I am growing uncomfortable in this environment. My encounters with management feel hurried, curt, and invalidating. By not checking in with Lea right before the conference, it is clear I have a problem with authority, they say. I must be a good for nothing anarchist. Their insistence on pointing out assumed wrongdoing and flaws in our character makes me and my peers lose focus and progressively shut down. It has been six months. What an ordeal! The honeymoon is over, and the silence in the office is ominous—oppressive, even. They lie routinely to our faces. They cheat also. It is the culture, they say when confronted. It is fair to say we are uneasy. I am dragging my feet to work, dreading any type of interaction with these sourpuss managers.

They spend large sums of money to scout and recruit the talented few crucial to the agency's mission. The vetting and on-boarding processes are complex. I am dissatisfied. All I can think about is leaving this Plantation—what else can I call this place? I know it will not be easy! The thought of repaying hiring bonuses is discouraging. It takes years to transform a traditional language instructor into an effective, versatile government trainer— someone able to support operations and deliver training for success in the field. The life and death of agents hang in the balance.

Every night, a mushroom plantation bum-rushes my nightmares. It has become an obsession. Mushrooms evoke fungus and dirt, dark and moist places. Mushrooms thrive on manure. Along with bacteria, fungi are crucial in the decomposition of organic matter. Most of my peers are treated like mushrooms. We are kept in the dark and covered in poop. We reek of it. And when we get too big for our britches, unceremoniously, we are kicked out and canned. Under that mushroom cloud, life looks bleak. The thought of quitting haunts me.

Some of us are sent to training to learn how to trust more; others are told that by remaining silent and not socializing, they are creating a hostile work environment. Managers make decisions about subordinates, without consulting us. We make our little contributions; they take the credit, get the kudos and flash their plastic smiles. They do not trust us, peons, individually or as a group, and do not bother developing us unless it proves politically expedient. To management, training is a reward to be dished out. The yeomen do all the work, keep the place afloat, and feel ignored. Mind over money. No one articulates an explicit leadership vision or anything lofty enough for us to buy into. We are run ragged. We know little of their plans and what else is going on in the organization, which encourages rumormongering. Yet, the lure of paychecks and bonuses ensures that the system lives on.

A few of my peers are singled out for attention and offered opportunities for development. Not me. I do not care anymore! I am on their shit list. The brownnosers are easy to spot. It is kind of hard to get rid of the smudge. These unscrupulous self-promoters are the fastest to move up the promotion ladder. The price they pay for managers' favors is exacting: long hours, late nights, weekend work. Becoming a yes-person would have taken a toll on me, my sense of integrity and all. I am stupid enough to insist on remaining true to myself. The pecking order has been defined. Not willing to pay the price, I plow along dispirited, not understanding how I fit into the larger picture, how to respond to the gnawing Gallup survey prompt "I know what is expected of me at work."

To varying degrees, my colleagues and I, we are growing fearful of management's shadow, and focusing on avoiding negative attention. Prolonged fear destroys self-confidence, creativity, motivation, and productivity. We are oppressed; we know it and feel depressed. An oppressed person exists only to be used as a tool by his tormentor. Having children to raise and a mortgage to pay makes it unwise to express an honest opinion. We are shrinking, becoming littler people. Even I, Antoine, a large, burly man is now fluttering about like a damsel in distress. Disagreeing with people feels self-indulgent. It is better to smile whenever it is impossible to lie. Artificial harmony prevails and sucks the air out of our brains, but the bills are getting paid. Thinking has become a luxury that few can afford. We little shrinking people do not want the responsibility of making tough decisions and confronting problems. We prefer to be told what to do. Self-accountability is not even a word, and it sounds so ugly.

In the face of blatant disrespect, I, like other employees, bristle, shut my mouth and endure. Once, a trainer disappeared never to be seen again. The stress, rumor had it, caused her to miscarry. To express dissent and alternative viewpoints was akin to career suicide. When people pretend to be small, the likelihood of runaway deadlines and project failures increases. With dirty managers, we were co-creating a culture of silence. Abuse loves silence.

Formal power brings out deference in unassertive employees. Our mindless deference to managers increases the probability that we will be abused. Through our meekness, obsequiousness and eagerness to please, we the mushrooms are contributing to the misbehavior of the poop slingers.

The school's mushroom managers rely on poor assumptions about what we are capable of, what we know, who we are, and what motivates us. They do not even bother to ask questions. I suppose we are too dumb! Maybe they know it all. They have too little time to spare. The enemy is within; it is a controlling mindset coupled with poor management practices, and it produces resentment.

Managers get compliance instead of commitment. What level of performance are they priming the pump for? What can they expect in terms of day-to-day performance? They form no human connections and give us no reason to care about them and the agency. Resentment and small-mindedness abound. What are they afraid of?

Younger, more resilient staff take turns planning ever-more-entertaining happy hours where everyone releases pent-up frustrations. The week's goings-on, office politics, and pettiness became sources of rib-splitting humor. Happy hours serve as escape valves. Without them, we soldier-ants, would have long abandoned the anthill.

During the end-of-year celebrations, the language school becomes a place of unity and unbridled joy. We party with abandon. Partying is serious business. It takes flavorful foods and wild international music to break down the walls of differences. Uninhibited, in the moment, trainers dance and tap into the deep joy we feel. We exist, at last. Christmastime feels like carnival. In our head, we can be whatever we want to be. Our contorting bodies oozing sweat offer a glimpse into repressed passions. We all shimmy rapturously to Arabian music. Managers wrapped in moral outrage, unswayed by the sensuality of the merrymaking, restrain themselves and hover. Their unspoken disapproval reinforces a common sense of identity among us. In the face of evil, we are one!

The party over, normalcy is restored. I find myself like many others, desperate, going along to get along. My attempts to fit in are met with stubborn denials. To make the pain go away, in the name of the paycheck, the temptation to disown my own voice, my confidence, and self-respect resurfaces. Some among us are transformed into zombies. They become visiting ghosts in their own lives. Work is war, it is political, and it is deadly. To survive, most absent their minds, put their hearts on mute and become spiritless shadows of their former selves…until the next celebration. To feel safe, we show up small and compromise our dreams of making a difference.

To dream of better working conditions

seems frivolous. The way we live—getting up before the crack of dawn, rushing to a building we've come to hate, dealing with people we no longer respect, performing jobs we have stopped believing in—we have convinced ourselves, is all for the better. The world over, parents lose their soul and sacrifice so their kids can thrive. We call that being mature.

Every four years, a study appears detailing the sorry state of diversity and inclusion in the upper echelons of the Plantation. Every four years, promises are made and speeches, delivered; money talks, and bullshit walks. Minority employees listen without enthusiasm, each time a little more dispirited, a little more checked out. The ploy works. Most personal ambitions are thrown into a dead sea of benevolence. The Plantation appears to care yet does nothing. What better way to underhandedly compound a problem? Exclusion by frustration is the order of the day. The way we do business. To act in earnest is to send waves of fear among undeserving managers. Poor babies, "They do the best they can", I am often told. Resignations follow, the self-selection out of ambition never fails, and those who stay, zone out. The process of valuing all individuals and leveraging their diverse talents is a stillborn pipe dream. The so-called force for change, too often, crushes the very people it is meant to help.

The few people whose actions demonstrate a genuine commitment to inclusion are left untapped. They will not join the ranks of managers. Mission first, biases and judgments before clear-mindedness and inquiry. That all-important ability to make fast decisions calls the shots and cuts corners. The fears of the chosen few and their mental models keep projecting a dim view of the world. A leadership of worms endures because sycophancy is leading the promotion process. A culture of superior execution and innovation shot down, sacrificed to the tyranny of the same old, same old. Sycophantic misleaders bent to the whims of pasty-faced power brokers add to the chaos of thoughtlessness.

A computer-based evaluation revealed to all on my team how students feel about each of us. A glitch in the computer system exposed our guarded vulnerabilities and destroyed what little trust there was left among us on the French team. Out of five, I come out first, ranked most effective. That welcome feedback spells my doom. Immediately, my teammates stop talking to me, stop including me in meetings and planned activities. The resentment of my peers and management's emphasis on group harmony above all else reinforce my feeling of alienation. Mediocrity, to the extent that it maintains team cohesion, is rewarded over superior performance. The bureaucrats aim for "good enough" and frown on performances that exceed expectations. I am being punished for doing exactly what I have been hired to do.

A week after the students' evaluations, I take a ten-minute break from class and return to my desk to send a quick email. No one sees me walk by; no one knows I'm at my desk. Our dean, an elderly woman, dashes in, looking for a young female colleague a couple of cubicles away. A tall Hermès-scarf-wearing, wiry brunette with a lazy eye and a forever absent smile, the dean's understated style betrays a Frenchness that her forty years stateside has not yet erased. She has clearly taken a liking to this particular instructor. Rumor has it; she is grooming her for a management position.

"There are a few black people from Howard University here to talk to us. Would you care to join me?"

"What do they want?"

"You know what niggers want. What else? Money, of course!"

I overhear the conversation between the dean and my teammate. I am floored. It forces me outside of the circle of relevance. It alienates me. The insult injures my sense of belonging and instantly makes me the "other." Overwhelmed, fighting the urge to jump out of my skin, caught between the fear of losing my mind and the fear of losing my job, I repress my knee-jerk inclination to confront the dean and cower instead in my chair, defeated. I know those voices, and, tingling with resentment, I slowly, robotically, force my distressed body to see who is speaking. I see their backs moving away toward the conference room. I cannot help but feel betrayed—like an outcast, even— and can no longer do what I had planned to do that day or concentrate at all. I am numb. Depleted. More than the comment, what eats me up inside for the full agonizing year that follows is how I cowered for lack of a snappy comeback. In that instant, I groveled and betrayed my own sense of morality!

I take to sitting and standing in an unbecoming hunchback posture, often neglecting to remove my coat and fidgeting constantly. To bolster the team's morale, the God-awful dean decides to no longer allow me in the classroom. In less than a week, I become more of an outsider, looking through a window into a calling that is being denied. What happened? Within a week, I have moved from purgatory into full-blown hell. My soul is bleeding. Just cannot get over it. All my conversations now end with the same litany: This job is killing me. There is nothing for me to do here. I am part of the so-called fight against terror. Lately, I am more terrorized of going to work. I cannot do this, and I cannot do that! I am bored out of my mind.

It's a cold morning. I'm freezing my ass off. Creeping behind a brush next to an alleyway, I have been staking the place since before sunrise. It's crazy how people don't mind keeping their curtains wide open for all to see inside. Never ceases to amaze me. I love it. I watch her from behind lock the door to her house. No one's home. Her husband and kids have been gone for thirty minutes now. I need to get to work. If I hurry, I could cut her throat before she gets to the car. In my dreams, I kill the old bitch a thousand times.

I feel a surge of adrenaline in my brain. Moving on, getting out of that hellhole has become my yearlong obsession. But I can't. I signed that damn agreement. Shame is triggering a steady change in me. Too bad. Insecure, authoritarian managers will just have to deal with it. They are gonna feel challenged. I am done being good. Fuck good. How about being real for a change? Real…as in a real nigga. 'cause that's all I am to them. A big nigger with a bald-head, and nothing else. But I am more than that.

Now, I am lashing out, standing tall, I no longer am a wallflower. I begin by asking too many questions. That is my way of restoring a sense of clarity. The little black mouse has left the building. I am a giant rat and I got teeth too. My newfound intense gaze, deep voice, divergent thinking, outspokenness, and effortless ability to command attention are all fast becoming disruptive. No more playing small, getting along to get along, being a nice, unthreatening chap, for what? To be pissed on? I wanna scare the bejesus out of their sorry asses. I find a sudden delight in the thought. I have lost respect for authority and totally stopped caring what people think of me. I am becoming compelling. I am scaring myself. I can feel it. My days on the Plantation are numbered.

I am now increasingly shunned. My utterly lonely presence highlights in my view the office's failure to embrace my difference. Many strive to unsee me—to become willfully blind to my humanity. Their cowardice makes me bigger, more powerful. I am fast becoming the center of their universe and I dwarf the cowards. They can keep talking about me for all I care! They belong to the in-group—to the mainstream, I belong to the fringes, the other side of the tracks; to try so hard and dismiss my compelling humanity is to precipitate your doom. I am the darkest brother and the most ominous too. Poor fool. In your psyche, my hue contains a threat of deep and far-reaching disruptive transformations. Prepare to face my fury!

My sleep is invaded by images of me falling off a cliff, and they further destabilize my soul; a recurrent nightmare I refuse to unpack. The powerlessness I feel is as intense as my resolve. I must be strong in the face of uncertainty. Disconnection, not belonging, affords one the freedom to no longer give a damn. And I don't give a damn. The job I work so hard for is not working for me. Out of the ashes, like a phoenix I will rise. I must believe my own delusions, if not I am lost. I will eventually strengthen my will and love myself as if my life depends on it, because it does, and in the meantime, indulge and wallow in my formative pain. I need my pain to make me strong and forge that will, so I commit. The managers have grown fearful of the raw power I embody, yet do not fully own. There is a threat and a promise in that power. And I commit to the struggle.

I am not buying it. A naïve observer will conclude that top leadership hears only the good-news stories the overseers tell. If such is the case, corrective action is inconceivable. Dysfunction exists under their watchful eyes. Certainly, group chiefs excel at framing difficulties in a positive light, but when people problems become pervasive, surely someone has to do something! Something else must be at work. Dysfunctions serve a useful purpose. They inject fear into the system. Fear keeps people in line. Could it be that top leadership tacitly encourages dysfunction? It ensures that surprises and disruptions are kept to a minimum. Fear is good for business. Fear of losing one's job, one's status, one's autonomy, one's connection to others, fear of losing face... Everybody plays hard not to lose. With predictability, order, routine, and in the silence of their fears, bureaucrats come alive and show their pettiness.

4

In the cafeteria at the end of the lunch we share, fearful, Leila announces that her suspicious two-timing husband wants to meet with me the next day. What's this about? The bastard is coming out of the woodwork. She does not know what he wants. Enough already! She'd attempted to introduce me to him, and he'd rejected the idea saying he already had enough friends. Not even the slightest desire to get acquainted. She has no idea of what he wants now, yet she's fretting.

Since I don't know what the meeting is about, I have picked a public place, a Starbuck's down the street. A safe bet. I find him there during lunchbreak, and I approach. Leila's husband is a giant. A man with no obvious charm—a monstrosity, really! Six foot six, 260 pounds, hulk-like and stern. He looks depressed. Poor thing! Clearly, the dude spends too much time at the gym. All muscles, perhaps no brain, his chiseled body and unsmiling face could run chills down any man's spine. Leila has expressed resentment over his treatment of her lately. The fellow seems unhinged. He's probably gulped too many cups of java already. I have to be on guard. Anything can happen.

He leaves my stretched-out hand hanging and with an accent thicker than mine launches into a diatribe. What a raving lunatic! Vociferous and offensive. I interrupt.

"Slow down dude! I can barely understand what you're saying!"

No wonder you can't handle any more friends, I think to myself.

He then has the nerve to yell out in the crowded establishment:

"Have you been fucking my wife?"

"What?!"

Taken aback, I lift an eyebrow. Has he lost his damn mind? I do not know if I should run or stay, act flattered or appalled. I feel sorrier for him than anything. He's just told the world he's a cuckold. Poor fuck.

"No way, buddy! That's crazy! Where the hell did you get that idea from?" Now, I too am getting loud.

"Don't lie to me, motherfucker. I got evidence."

The jackass is bluffing. I would have known if I had done such a thing and not been here.

The patrons look uncomfortable. They give us more space and keep all eyes on us. Some look downright worried, others, amused.

Some are even giggling. Probably out of sheer nervousness. This is no laughing matter. People die over shit like that. Violence is lurking, rearing its ugly head. Black on black crime, this time over a white girl. *Qué lastima!* We are both standing tall, defiantly checking each other out. If I lose my life, at least he's got to give up an eye. I've had enough of the nonsense. I am motioning towards the door.

"Wait a minute," the cuckold yells. "Sorry. It's just … I've found emails my wife sent to her friends. None addressed to you, but she describes how she feels about you and the things she'd do to you."

"Why you bugging, man? I dunno shit about this. I'm not the one, son. Got nothing goin' on with your wife. Stop aggravating. I'm really pissed right now. Can't take any more of this bull."

"Listen. I'ma divorce her ass. I'm glad you got nothing to do with this shit. Don't get caught up in it, you hear. You might regret this."

Back at work, Leila has some explaining to do. She set me up! And she needs to come clean.

"Your husband is the sorriest son of a bitch I've ever met. What did you do, and why am I mixed up in it?"

"I'm so sorry, Antoine. He installed something on my computer at home, and the way I understand it, when I'm not around, he's able to go over everything I've typed on the keyboard."

"You and I have never exchanged emails or texts, at least not as far as I know. Right?"

"Right. But I really do have a thing for you, and he found out about it that way."

"A thing for me? You trying to get me killed? That son of a bitch is dangerous, you know."

"I'm so sorry."

She looks relieved and dumb. After such public humiliation and unjust accusation, I am shaken and flattered all at once. Brother, I swear, you will be a cuckold. You don't know it yet. Just you wait! Given the chance, indeed, it'll be my pleasure to exact sweet revenge.

5

Just by changing the way I think about setbacks, I'm becoming more resilient. Instead of letting frustration get the better of me, like colleagues, when I'm not promoted, I thank my lucky star for granting me so much money for so little effort. I cannot run away just yet. I need to survive the oppressive environment of the plantation. Creativity is the key to that growing resilience. My imaginary friends are very talkative. They prompt me to assign a crooked meaning to the most rotten of happenings. Fear is the opposite of creativity. Creativity is the key to my liberation. I have no ambition, no fear of failure, no risk aversion, and no fear of success. Now, I seek only to enlarge my experience. Neglect has introduced risk into my life and made me a failure. I have nothing to lose.

Leaving the language school is not going to be easy. Yet, I finally manage that desperate feat with the help of Diane, a miracle worker, the chief of workforce strategy and development. She negotiated my release. Thank God almighty. I am free at last. Free at last. Or so I think. Her office is on the sixth floor, and the language school on the fourth—too close for comfort but still, I'll manage. Diane offers me a position as program manager for instructor development, a step up for a broken man. I immediately start working for her in a newly formed five-person office set up to promote employee engagement. Lucky me, I am getting another lease on life. There is hope!

Whenever she initiates contact, Diane's big, deep, soft blue Mormon eyes smile at us. She welcomes us with open arms and positive expectations. If Jesus were a woman, he would have been Diane, tearing into my now closed impenetrable face.

Somebody please, tell this woman to stop looking at me like that! Her gentle demeanor could comfort a wolf, let alone a restless soul like mine. The pale skin, blond hair, and easy smile stand out in an unsmiling crowd. She scares me!

I had almost forgotten white people could be so kind. The lady has a heart, and she is melting the ice in my chest; melting away my reservations. I, like everyone around, love her strength, upbeat personality, and quieting presence. We trust her.

I am in denial. I find no solace in monthly one-on-one chats with her. There is no hiding place. She explores my feelings and thoughts, as she does with everyone. Has us talking about what is important to us in and outside of work. She opens up our lives as if we were books and shifts our moods like a witch would. She gets under my skin with insightful questions and gentle prodding; places me in the center of my story, never as the victim, always as the driver. No solutions, no advice given! She helps me think. Silence does the heavy lifting and makes for a beautiful experience. Content to ask provocative questions, she triggers new thoughts in me I am willing to own.

"Cry if you must cry." Strangely, she is kind and stern at the same time. How is that even possible? Arms spread wide open, resting on the backs of adjoining chairs, as if she owned the place, displaying grit, she digs into our inner turmoil, bringing the filth to the surface, in the open. "Do not wallow but stay in the fire until the heat subsides." What a strange creature! Diane is the real deal. The emotional connection between her and us is the key to our great performances. Deep faith, too. "When people care about people, they care back," she says. "People act more responsibly when we give them more responsibility."

Working with Diane feels like having a blank canvas to draw on, and a place for my imagination to run wild. There is nothing to fear, only faith and learning, never failure. I've already won. Training trainers, managing instructor certifications, creating events to energize the workforce are the staples of my day.

My brain is brimming with new ideas that shape monthly events that energize the workforce; disruptive ideas that shift people's perspectives and cause them to commit to the work of bettering themselves. My learning events are anticipated, relevant, funny, and thought provoking. They have a common thread: overcoming workplace dysfunctions, empowering oneself, leveraging one's potential. Bureaucracy is a bore.

I run the sessions like a Baptist preacher animated by faith, with great conviction, living the life. I was meant to do this. Because they did not want my efforts to go unnoticed, many provided feedback directly to Diane.

"Apparently, people are starved for intellectual stimulation."

"Say what, boss?"

"How do you do it? What do you do specifically to get such consistently high praises from participants in your events?" She's flattering me!

"I dunno. I guess, for inspiration, I listen

to them—to the noise they make, their whispers, what they say, and what they don't say. Then I deliver what they expect. I tie the presentations to their actual concerns and interests. Real learning is always learning about self, anyway."

"Listening's paid off, then."

"Using marketing tricks and presenters who have something to say, I gave voice to voiceless women, minorities, young and old people, the isolated, the disenfranchised, and rapidly developed a following."

"At last, doing this, I found my voice. To me, having a voice means having the ability to make an impact. When I stopped being afraid, I realized I was no longer a mere cog in a wheel. I grew bigger, took more initiative, and got more done. From the initial fifteen attendees you saw; each event now attracts hundreds of people. I'm rewriting my story, and reinventing myself. It's exciting."

"I guess you're right. I've now become your personal secretary. My phone's always ringing. People are energized after your events and always calling me to find out when the next one's scheduled, before it's even planned. They wouldn't be doing that if you weren't touching a nerve."

"Participants talk freely, speak their minds, let off steam, until they transform their pent-up frustrations into creative energy and forward movement. By challenging them to revisit their assumptions, we provoke thought."

"You've become a catalyst. I give you a platform and you give it to people as an outlet for self-expression. Based on the feedback, it's causing engagement to increase."

"That's wonderful news."

"And that is really all there is to it, right?"

"What can I say? They're great people, boss. Again, participation increases because they connect with the topics. I make room for their voices, expect a lot from them, and encourage alternate points of view, all of which in turn leads to higher engagement. They like that. It's intellectually stimulating. We keep it real. My speakers have something significant to share. There's a lot of pain here! You showed me that yourself, Boss."

"I guess then leadership is about how we relate to others, whether we view them as real people with a brain, aspirations, and a voice, not as objects. That's what I'm learning from you, young man."

"Just like you, I see their humanity, boss. There's no going back, I made the choice to show up with my values. Indeed, it's in the relationship that leadership lives."

6

After the divorce, Leila is floating on air. A monstrous weight of guilt has lifted. At the language school, she is gliding above the familiar currents of discontent.

"Happiness much like unhappiness is a state of mind, she says. It's all relative! The choice is ours."

How can she say that? Her ex made out with a big chunk of her inheritance. How is she even able to keep it together? In her shoes, I would have lost my marbles.

"It's only money," she says.

Yeah, right. Only money! With that money, I would have known just where to go and what to do. No doubt. She's rid of the drama, and that's all that matters. She breathes again, she says. Me, I'd be choking again in my own fury!

"There are bigger and better things to look forward to," she says.

The girl is from outer space! As unassertive as she appears, she remains hopeful. I need whatever drug she is on.

Handy around the house—she loves doing things with her own hands—she's pleasant as can be, rich and pretty too. What a combination? That broad is a G.O.A.T. the greatest of all times. How I wish she'd been a sista. That would have assuaged the guilt I feel sometimes.

She wants small talk.

"Don't bore me with politics and your theories, Antoine. You have too many," she says.

She's gonna get small talk.

"I'm pragmatic, not very intellectual. I read a lot nonetheless—romance novels, which I prefer to watching TV. No one is perfect. Hiihii. I love cooking gourmet meals, exercising, spending time with you, dancing, and laughing. These are my favorite things to do. What's not to like? Got a problem with that, Antoine? I ain't bad at all! Admit it, you dig me."

Time flies. As soon as the fun begun, it ended. For two fun-filled years, Diane made work on the Plantation fulfilling. Her tour has just come to an abrupt end. With her at the helm, my back has gotten straighter, my head has grown bigger.

The day after she left, an old geezer replaced her. A stickler for rules, untrusting, and anxious, the stiff established new procedures immediately, narrowed the scope of my work, and defined more conservative guidelines and outcomes. Does he want to keep me from continuing to do what I have been doing to great acclaim? Is he messing with me? In the blink of an eye, all autonomy is gone. The fool attempts to control my every move. Memories of restrictions and invalidations are rushing back to crush what is left of my spirit. I just cannot live in that space anymore. Not with him or anybody else! I am now desperately seeking a way out of this predicament, I feel doomed. Defeated. The work of the imagination has stopped. I cannot become a robot, once again. I refuse to be complicit in that madness. What choice do I have? My name is not Leila. The enemy is real, not a figment of my imagination! This is not a mere state of mind for me.

My three-year tour is finally coming to an end. Not a day too soon. Free at last, I can leave. Diane has been gone a whole year! With no clue where to go next, I have to be careful, and make sure that I too interview the next boss that'll be interviewing me. I got to find the right fit. Can no longer leave things up to chance. What is chance, anyway? Got nothing to do with me. I learned my lesson the hard way. Now, I anticipate a more complete transformation at the next assignment. Geographic distance may provide the best opportunity for my continued growth. What do I want? Security, a salary, and stimulation.

Who am I kidding? That cannot be all. What about status, certainty, autonomy, relatedness, and fairness as well? These are nonnegotiable. I'm a hog. I want it all. Not only have I gained clarity, but a higher purpose as well. My work speaks for itself. I have a brand and a reputation to uphold, now. I add value to people's lives. What I stand for is clear: change. I'm a troublemaker with conviction.

Another group is considering me for a new position as program manager for leadership development. I am being pursued. They like my independent streak and advocacy for greater employee empowerment. This time, choosing to be vocal has proved beneficial. The Center for Technology Exploitation wishes to hire me because of my "hall file" (what people say about me behind my back) and not in spite of it. A hall file can make or break a career.

7

Even though I have moved on, Leila clings to me with the help of a new routine. I live alone thirty minutes away from her. Having no particular culinary skills, I eat out all the time. She knows that I cannot boil an egg to save my life. In the kitchen, I often forget something's cooking and am tired of throwing food away. Now, she insists I stop over on the way home.

"The least I could do is to satisfy your appetite. We should help each other out," she says.

Leila is luring me. To be sure, I'm basically making it easy for her. The wench is hiding a secret that is making her feel insecure. With the help of foundation, as skillfully as she can, she camouflages an onset of melanoma.

During the interview, Teresa, the new boss relates what my previous manager said about me:

"You should not hire him if you want someone that'll agree with everything you say. If, on the other hand, you want to know exactly what he thinks, he'll tell you the truth you need to hear, and not the truth you wish to hear."

"Call me crazy. My professional

challenges are daunting." She reassures me, "I can ill afford a yes-man, again."

I am pleased and can release my breath.

Majestic, the new building dwarfs all the surrounding facilities. It stands in the middle of a large parking lot. Newly built and richly appointed, a ponderous calm emanates from it. The high ceilings; the fancy, oversized elevators; the wide, shiny halls; the inescapably modern feel of the place; the tiled granite walls; and the discreet metallic touches all make it look sleek and coolly cerebral.

There is a geeky quality to this place. It is refreshing. On the roof, solar panels, antennas, and cameras reinforce the high-tech feel. Glass panels allow abundant light to filter in. Tall, healthy plants and wide aisles create an airy, almost organic atmosphere.

The Office of Training is co-located with Human Resources and Personnel in a large, luminous vault on the eighth floor. People smile here and dress more casually than in the old building. They are brimming with joy, giddy with excitement, I am taking it all in. For fear of a sugar coma, I must steer clear of the common area. It is replete with donuts, cookies and pies.

Her voice is a bark, too loud for the office. She is the life of the party. Hyper, a cheerleader at heart, though she tries, Teresa barely succeeds in hiding a thick Southern drawl. Born and raised in Tennessee, she stands at five foot five inches.

Her single mission in life is to make us believe she cares. The woman is a hoot. When sedate, she manages a less inflected speech. Her desk remains covered with treats. She must have a sweet tooth. Her body bears the mark of that indulgence. Not that I wanted to see it, loose skin hangs over her skirt. She's flabby.

Her sad droopy eyes make me believe she's lonely. People say that after a whirlwind romance, she married late in her thirties, gave birth to a son, and became a widow by her late forties. Cancer doesn't care!

I am the only staffer. The team is made up of contractors. Shahila, Lorie, Stacey, and Brian are the trainers I will be relying on to deliver my program. Stacey appears open and humble. A tall blond in her fifties with a beaming smile, a former coach and Pennsylvania beauty queen, she draws me in immediately. Stacey has recently married an engineer from across the hall because, she says, he was relentless.

"Why is she telling me that? I don't care."

I must understand, the consummate team player, she wants nothing more than for our teammates to get along, she says.

"Unlike others, I know how to keep my ego in check."

"Good to know," I reply. She wants me to join a fitness class she teaches on the premises.

"I'm freaking out. Is she attempting to tell me something?"

Shahila is more reserved, less forward than Stacey. An Indian from Uganda, African by birth, Canadian by adoption, and American by choice. Because she loves Central America, she fancies herself a Latina. With a degree in education, besides me, she is the only real educator in the lot. They migrated to Canada after Idi Amin Dada expelled her family from Uganda in the 1970s.

As an adult, in the 1980s, she worked as a teacher-trainer in Nicaragua; married an American before being ousted, this time by the Sandinistas. She followed her husband back to the United States and raised two sons. Scrappy, Shahila is still a force of nature in her sixties. She tells stories with a punch. Far from a fairy tale, her life has never been easy nor boring!

At twenty-nine, Brian is the youngest in the group. He navigates the maze of strong personalities with ease, making us feel as if we are his friends. Born and raised in a wealthy suburb of northern Virginia, he's lived a sheltered life isolated from other African Americans. Growing up his biggest struggle was confronting an upper-middle-class dad with bipolar disorder. He seems well adjusted, self-assured, and focused on providing great service. The man's a pleaser!

Lorie, a matronly woman with a sluggish disposition, keeps her large behind glued to a comfortable chair all day. In her late sixties, she retired as a staff employee and got rehired the next day as a contractor.

While she wears the title "senior trainer" with pride, she refuses to cooperate with the likes of me. Everyone says she cannot be outdone at doing close to nothing. In government, she reckons, no one will make her do anything she does not want to do; and no one has the heart to try, either. She must be right! When I request to meet with her and the rest of the team to discuss how the work will be divvied up, Lorie refuses to join us. She wants no part in that conversation. Totally unprepared for such resistance and frankly taken aback, I leave her alone. The boss ought to take care of this foolishness. I have no teeth or assigned authority and dealing with problem employees is above my pay grade. "What lie must she have told to get the job?" I wonder.

8

There is no time to sit around and catch one's breath the first day on the job. Teresa insists on taking me to all the managers' meetings she is scheduled to attend. I must speak my mind, weigh in and not be shy, she insists. Her peers come across as a jolly weird bunch. After a warm welcome, they each articulate high expectations of me.

Intimidated, all the while, I keep my eyes down and readjust my collar a few times. I am not used to positive expectations. It turns out, they consider me Teresa's deputy. Officially, no one's told me anything of the sort. I fear I may be exposed as a troublemaker. At the third meeting, I finally open my mouth and provide insight. A heavy silence ensues. All twenty people assembled look flabbergasted. What have I done? A question they have been wrestling with has finally been answered. There are gasps of relief about me. The stupor evaporates. The flutter and the humming resume. The interest makes me feel warm and fuzzy. I am not used to that.

At the fourth meeting, the executive director takes me aside and apprizes me of an issue she wants addressed.

"Should Devin, the director, go, the front office, would be unable to maintain a style of leadership that has worked well for the center." I listen intently.

"We've been pushing a bold agenda on a dubious workforce. Managers at every level are too transactional. No one is transformational enough. To the admonitions to take more risks, push the envelope, and promote innovation, middle managers reactions are at best timid. They either lack the know-how, or focus too much on the constraints and what cannot be done. The right climate for innovation has to be nurtured. It takes transformational leaders to build an organization's capacity to engage in the innovation process."

Why is she telling me this? I am quite sold on the concept already. Before joining the Plantation, I had worked for two transformational leaders. I can barely contain my excitement. What is she expecting from me?

"Confused and torn between the director's ask and their supervisors' resistance, the workforce does not know what to do. Our culture needs an upgrade. Technology is driving the need for change. A technology center, be it private or public, must innovate. The status quo is no longer acceptable.

Antoine, we've been following you. You are what we call an influencer. We need your help to sell the upgrade."

What an honor! I think. She considers me up to the task! In effect, the executive director is giving me license to kick ass. And that, I am always ready to do!

9

Intent on making an impression, every time I visit, Leila is outdoing herself in the kitchen again. She knows what she wants and spares no effort to get it. We clicked the minute we met. To her, I am the real deal. Frankly, it's flattering. I dunno why she thinks so highly of me, but I don't really care why. All that matters is what she says: "She has to be with me because I am the one."

Hello!

Misfits in a pod of drones, we are children of divorces. I grew up shaking dreadlocks to the sound of Bob Marley and the Wailers. She was raised in a community of hippies, with parents on a never-ending quest for nirvana, a French father and an American mother high on life. I was a rude boy and she, a naughty girl. We share a common experience of teenage angst and rebellion. The business clothes we wear feel like poor attempts at redemption. They make us look awkward in the stuffy environment of the plantation.

Angelic as she now appears, Leila evades notice more easily than I can. Less assured, less dominant than me, the vulnerability she displays is her ticket to acceptance into the herd. She is a woman among women, Pretty and well bred, one they can identify with. She looks cultured, and oozes an "old France" flair that arouses nostalgia in others, yet she feels no special bond with the old country or its admirers. A part of her refuses to belong and strives for the shadows. Her friends come from elsewhere, anyplace but here. She doesn't belong in this masquerade. In the office, I seem to be the only one who is aware of that small fact. Others assume she is an easy mark for my lewd advances, me the predator, when in fact, she is a darker horse than they will ever guess! Why must I always be the bad guy?

The week after I started, I must attend a three-day management off-site, a retreat in Maryland, hours away. I am tasked to observe and take notes because I am to take over the design and facilitation of the offsites in the months to come.

"Managers are an indecisive bunch," Teresa says. "Yet their input is essential to the front office decision-making process. It is needed on a number of issues only they have direct knowledge of."

She is assisting Mark, the chief of operations —a taller, younger version of Paul Newman—with the facilitation. Stacey is providing logistical support. A splendid, rustic, art-filled Chesapeake waterfront mansion minutes away from an outlet mall serves as the ideal location for the meeting. The stately pines; well-manicured lawns; spacious, high-ceilinged, elegant rooms, and intricate leatherwork enhance my mood. There is a Ralph Lauren quality to that place—a debonair formality that matches my usual disposition. I feel grand!

Staring blankly, donning somber moods, dragging their feet all the way to their seats, participants trickle in for the one-thirty in the afternoon start of the event. Dull, unknown people are sucking the stale air out of the huge, impersonal conference room. The stiffs look bored already. The event hasn't even begun yet.

Without a clear sense of what success looks like, Teresa and Mark start doing what they believe is best. I am disturbed by the level of their incompetence. Who said anyone could facilitate a meeting? But they are my superiors, so I keep my trap shut.

I am not amused. Mark fails to provide clear directions during the facilitation, gets easily distracted and does not finish the sentences he begins. He balks at unexpected comments, changes course midway, and responds hastily to unfinished questions. Red faced and defeated; he turns to Teresa begging to be rescued. With a dejected look each time, she steps in and fires questions at the confused audience, waits a second or two, then answers her own questions.

What a ghastly scene! I wonder why the managers are putting up with the charade. Why don't they just all walk out? Teresa and Mark provided no agenda and hurried through a big nothing. The managers are pursing their lips, lowering their gazes, frowning, fidgeting, and repressing their growing irritation, faking smiles, fighting to curb devilish impulses yet they keep putting up with the fraud. On occasions, someone heaves a loud sigh of annoyance which causes Mark once again to modify an activity on the spot.

At around two o'clock on the following Friday, the retreat ends. Not an hour too soon. All is well again, at last. No one looks more relieved than Mark and Teresa. Another box has been checked. Without fanfare, people check out of their rooms, and rush to their cars to get home.

No one volunteers to stay behind and help tidy the conference room. Stacey had arranged to hitch a ride back to Virginia with me. It takes a while before we finally leave. We both hurry and trash the leftover materials, pick up the papers and cups scattered all over desks, and straighten what needs to be straightened, tables and chairs, before making our way out the door.

10

It is bright out. Despite the frigid air, the sun is beaming. Stacey and I make an odd pair: a curvaceous, full-bosomed figure tagging along with a stout, broad-shouldered, jittery hunk of a man twenty years her junior. Who would have thought? The coy expression on her face, her slightly tilted head make her seem sweet and delicate, while it makes me seem intense and protective.

My imagination is getting the better of me now. I like mature women. The shyness in her prissy smile hints at a forbidden whim, one she strives to repress. Doubt mixed with fear and a desire to please oozes out of our awkward glances. Self-restraint feels like violence, a perfect disguise for our impulses. What are we anticipating? We size each other up before convening on the safest way to engage.

"What did you think of the retreat?" I say first, tentatively.

"Well, I thought it went okay. A little weird but okay! Ever since Mark took it over, it's not been, you know, as good as it used to be."

"Who used to run it?"

"John, the former chief of operations. A

very confident and dynamic guy. You don't know him. I'll point him out to you."

"Have you been supporting the off-site for a long time?"

"Been involved with it ever since it began five years ago. We started after the director asked all employees, 'If you were the director for a day, what would you change?'"

"What did people respond?"

"There were so many responses that he decided we should get the managers together, have them go through them one by one, and determine what was actionable and what wasn't. People were excited at first and put a lot of effort into it at the time."

"What came of it?"

"Lots of new initiatives. We've been holding off-sites ever since. Soon enough, you'll see how important they really are."

As she reminisces, Stacey is opening up and smiling at me mischievously. Doesn't she know she's in danger? That smile of hers arouses me. Men are indeed predictable creatures and I am a slut.

The road is long. After placing our bags in the trunk, we start down the windy dirt lane that leads to the highway. Stacey and I start bobbing our heads in unison to the loud music coming from the radio. We both relish British pop and feel a connection in the moment. She smiles brighter, exuding happiness. I am averting my eyes, trying to deflate an erection before she notices. She thinks me down to earth, approachable and easy to talk to. I am only showing interest in what she has to say, trying to control my nature.

"No one's cared enough to lend a helping hand and tidy up before. That makes you different, if not better than most, Antoine."

Right about now, she really should be careful with the compliments. I am bursting with desire.

"Can I be honest with you? I want you to succeed in this new assignment, Antoine. There are a few things you should know before you can, though. Everything looks fine on the surface, but in reality, we have huge problems on the team."

"I hear you!"

"I mean it! Ever since some people that shall remain nameless joined the team, things have been going downhill. We fight over stupid stuff. Nothing gets done anymore. I worry that unless someone puts their foot down, things will get worse."

"What exactly are you talking about?"

"I don't wanna get anyone in trouble, but

since Shahila was hired, team morale's gone down. She's not a team player. She doesn't share or communicate at all. She hogs the spotlight and tries to take credit for everything. I'm sick of it. She needs to get fired. Always sucking up to the bosses. I guess that's why they don't have a clue about her and what she's really about."

"What's she really about?"

"She's all about herself."

I am getting an earful I did not ask for. Stacey proceeds to recite all the ways in which Shahila is not hacking it. She lists the wrongs she has done! At that point, the trip becomes more tedious than it needs to be.

Enough. I get it. Stacey wants Shahila out—that is crystal clear already. She feels threatened. For the first time in a long time, she's facing a formidable competitor, a source of angst. The more she talks about Shahila, the more she reveals herself. The more she exposes another's flaws, the more she reveals her own. Assigning flaws to others provides deeper insights into who the finger-pointer is.

I listen begrudgingly, while Stacey yammers away uninterrupted for close to an hour, searching for the reason I had found her attractive to begin with. I must have momentarily lost my mind since I cannot recall any. I cannot handle this much complaining anymore. I finally interrupt her when the car crosses the bridge over the Potomac that separates Maryland from Virginia.

"How have you contributed to the problems on the team? And how exactly have you tried to address the issues with Shahila?"

The questions befuddle her. She mutters something inaudible, breathes loudly, and then demands I turn up the music. Now Stacey is ignoring me, acting like I don't exist. She expected sympathy and some kind of a promise of action. In her eyes, I have power. How flattering!

Stacey's assessment of Shahila cannot become the definitive story of Shahila. Superficial assessments of me had me labeled "not a team player", "talkative", "crazy", "critical", "self-doubting", and "intense". Given the limitations of my former team, I wanted to believe that I could achieve success faster and more reliably by going it alone, and this could also mean that I was laser focused on achieving results. I cared little of what people thought of me, which makes me very independent. I choose to believe that being talkative is my way of being sociable. When someone calls me crazy, I believe that that person does not understand my forward-thinking, creative ways. It is all in the reframe!

To say that I am critical is to acknowledge that I do not shy away from using critical-thinking skills even when others wish I would not. When I sometimes exhibit self-doubt, I take it to mean that I am comfortable showing vulnerability. To the charge of being intense, I counter that I care very much about what I do.

These criticisms have a flip side. There is no telling what those labels ultimately reveal! Believing my own truths afford me a way of detaching from the limiting beliefs of others. I taught myself to accept criticism only from people I trust. I am nobody's fool. I will sit down with Shahila before I accept Stacey's assessment of her.

11

The week following the managers' off-site, Teresa is tasking the training team with designing, organizing, and providing logistical support for a high-visibility conference hosted annually by the front office. It will enable the Center to highlight its successes and to introduce its products to hundreds of potential users. Devin, the director, will be addressing two hundred officers. We have a three months head start, yet, two months after being tasked and a month before the big day, we have completed all major arrangements.

Whenever they speak in public, managers like sycophants play up the great man and his vision. Through his efforts, employee engagement has been increasing, they say. I've heard so much about the man, I can barely wait to hear him speak in person and find out what the hype is all about.

The Technology Orientation Course (TOC 101), a mandatory three-day on-boarding course, provides an overview of what the Center does, the scope of its efforts, and its mission. My team runs it with Shahila at the helm. This week, I am in attendance.

I'm so bored, I fall asleep. Now more than

ever, I look forward to having a chat with Shahila. Next Thursday seems like the perfect time to do it. To suggest improvements to the training we run is one of my responsibilities. At nine o' clock, sharp, I'm ready to go. A few hours later, Shahila finally makes time for our chat.

"Thanks for meeting with me. How ya doin'?"

"Fine, sir. How're you?" She stretches her legs.

"Not bad. Not bad, at all." I'm now stretching my legs too.

"I wanted to talk to you about TOC 101."

"What 'bout it? I was surprised by you, sir," she says with a smirk. "You brought food to the room. You know full well it's against the rules. And, to add insult to injury, you dozed off in the middle of class."

"Well, I was hungry. I forgot about that rule," I sheepishly respond, scratching my head. "But I was really taken aback myself. That class isn't what I expected at all. It was a lil'—"

"I'm sorry, sir. The evals are excellent. People love it. Since I took it over, I've received nothing but kudos from the front office and participants. You should have seen it before. Lorie and Stacey ran the damn thing into the ground. They wouldn't tell me what I needed to know. I figured it all out anyway. You should be thanking me instead of criticizing."

"Clearly, you have passion. There's no question you do a great job making sure everything runs smoothly. That's impressive. You care very much—obviously. But do you really believe this qualifies as training?"

"Whatever do you mean?" Shahila's aggravation is palpable.

"You had twelve presenters, right?"

"That's the way we've always done it. Every group needs an opportunity to present the work they do."

"I understand that. What I mean is, can we make those presentations more memorable, exciting, and interactive too? And help the presenters figure out whether their information is resonating with the audience?"

"I've tried that already; they've included my suggestions. It's hard to get those people to do more than what they're already doing."

"Why is that, Shahila?"

"Teaching is not their cup of tea. They have real jobs, you know. And they get tasked at the last minute. You never know in advance who'll be available."

"That's no way to deliver a course."

"Sir, I do my best. I'm quite successful, considering. What are you trying to say?"

"Yes, yes, I agree. You do a great job. However, some things must change if this is to qualify as training."

"It's training," Shahila yells in a feisty tone.

"I know everyone around here wants to believe that; however, there were no learning objectives, no assessments of learning, and no student interactions. To me, that was more like a series of briefings. No one wants to be talked at for hours, several days in a row. That's painful. I couldn't take it. That's why I dozed off."

"Sir, with all due respect, it's clear you don't appreciate the hard work I do around here. Again, this course has received excellent evaluations. The front office is happy with it."

"Shahila, this has nothing to do with you doing a bad job. I'm saying that the briefers should change their style, or we might as well call this what it is: a series of briefings, furthermore..."

"We're done here. I gotta go." Shahila abruptly turns around and rushes out of sight.

Really?

12

Leila seems mesmerized. Could it be my deep-set eyes? She stares into them all the time when I'm around. It's freaking me out. She would, for hours, if I allowed it. After gazing at me, she feels inclined to surrender every inch of her womanhood. I am a lucky bastard.

As if possessed, she longs for the touch that will quiet her trepidations, the thrusts that will threaten to tear her asunder. Minutes feel like lifetimes, then she collapses on my chest and inhales the sweet perfume of my pungent sweat married to her own. I am a carnivore. Too much meat's not good for me! Satisfied, she smiles an ingenuous smile. Separation is jarring. She wants me to linger. I suffer from delusions.

Yes, Leila is growing on me. There is much I like about her. For one, she does not ask too many questions. People first notice her coy smile. I first noticed the bold, shapely curves she tries so hard to hide. Bottom heavy, tender and sweet, with a long tapering neck, she's built like a Bosc pear, and dresses inexpensively yet with flair. Light on top, dark on the bottom, the raised waist falling right below the bustline shifts the focus to the top of her body. How could she be the frumpy type? Style does not equate to money. To give off a classy vibe, she thinks pearls, cotton, wool, linen and silk.

Easy-going no matter the situation, Leila maintains her cool and knows how to keep her mouth shut. She wants to belong, to be loved, and protected. Who doesn't? Kind to a fault, this is what I love most about her. She cannot tell a lie to save her life.

Of the four homes she owns, three are rental properties located in prime urban locations. Disciplined with money, she never wastes any. It is fair to say, delicate and serious, she has the makings of a great catch. Thing is, I'm not on the market. Certainly not for a committed relationship. If I were, she might play me like she did her husband. I don't wanna be pussy-whipped or suffer a cuckold's agony.

My legs are long. The compact car she drives reminds me how frugal she is. I will not be caught dead in a thing so small. I tried it, and hated the experience. She got on my case once for spending five bucks on a cup and offered to make me coffee every morning instead. Even with other people's money, Leila is a miser.

In her sweet way, she thinks I'm a fool. "It's unreasonable to overpay for things," she belches. To keep the peace, I started saving pennies.

I've been observing Brian. I marvel at how impeccable his dress and manners are at all times; his speech is positive to a fault and smacks of political correctness. What a square! Very diplomatic, he graciously excuses bad behavior in others. His cautiousness makes him predictable. People like him, though; I kind of like him too, but I think he's a phony. Likeability ensures people want him around. There's worst. He's not too bad for a square! He anticipates our needs, offering a response before a request is even made—an attitude probably motivated by the fear of losing his job. With four mouths to feed at home, who could blame him? Unemployment is a luxury most people cannot afford.

Despite a rocky relationship, his parents had managed to keep the family together. Brian wishes to do the same. As a kid, he acted as a buffer between his mom and dad, and felt responsible for his father's mood swings and tried hard not to provoke him. Whenever his mother showed sadness, he comforted her, making amends for the sins of his father. Born into a system, he played a role that he still performs today outside of that system. On the team, he also serves as a buffer. The same role he has always played.

His stay-at-home girlfriend was pregnant two years in a row, and gave birth back-to-back. The boys, now five and six, look just like him. A consummate family man, although not the biological father, Brian was proud of his teenage daughter. He and I couldn't be more different.

One mustn't acknowledge setbacks but maintain a façade at all times. "What will people think? Avoiding the appearance of dysfunction matters today as much to him as it did to his mother. T'is better to inspire envy rather than pity! What an exhausting life, downright stressful!

Alone in satisfying everyone's needs, Brian struggles to maintain the sense of autonomy he longs for in the pursuit of his passion for script-writing—a solitary endeavor that calls for a great deal of space and time. Every minute counts. His time is no longer his own. He craves the illusion of freedom. The ride to work provides an opportunity to listen to the books he otherwise would have no time to read; lunch breaks, an opportunity to edit the writing he completes after waking each morning. Brian dreams of movies and glory, of proving his worth, and of working on his craft full time.

Mustering pleasantries, in the morning, he greets everyone with a flattering comment before settling down to work. In a stuffy office, he is like a breath of fresh air. Why can I not be more of a gentleman, like Brian? I don't want to. Simple enough answer.

When not causing people to smile, he lays low in his cubicle, never interferes with the bad blood between Shahila and Stacey and appears to not take sides. When people start complaining, Brian smiles and excuses himself. The man's too good to be true. Steering clear of the politics, seeing himself as a good guy, and working hard to maintain his stellar reputation, when arguments come to a head, shucking and jiving like an escape artist, he's the first one out the door. I ain't buying his act. That goody two shoes bastard is definitely playing a part in the dysfunction in the office. His silent avoidance encourages mayhem.

On a slow day, I invite him to lunch to find out what his deal is.

"Thank you for giving me this opportunity to get to know you better, man."

"Oh, don't mention it."

"I thought we should talk, away from the office. You're probably wondering what I'm planning to do with the team," I say before he asks, nibbling on some lettuce. I need to lose weight.

"Yeah, of course. But I know you only got here…what, a few months ago? You're probably still figuring things out."

"You're right, I am. But even at this early stage, it's important for you to know what I have in mind! We're a team, right?"

"I guess you're right," Brian says, chomping on a piece of pizza.

"I have a vision of what I want to accomplish here with you guys."

"Oh yeah? What is it?"

"I want our team to provide the type of training that others want to emulate throughout the Center. I want us to become the go-to people for best practices in training around here and beyond."

"That sounds great. You have your job cut out for you, right?"

"Well, yeah. I've noticed, and that's partly why I wanted to get together."

"Count me in, though. I like a challenge. I've always wanted to be more involved with classroom training. That's what I thought the job was about. It turns out it's more about providing logistical support to other people's training."

"Yeah, I've noticed that too. That needs to be addressed. We can't have instructors only spending their time running rosters and slides, making copies for others, opening and closing doors, and supplying drinks and snacks to students. We can do more. That's nice and helpful but a huge waste of talent, don't you think?"

"I'm glad you think so, too. Our team hasn't really trained in ages. If you don't mind my asking, why do you care about this so much?"

"Funny you should ask, since that's exactly what I wanted to find out from you—what you care about. I'll answer your question first, though. My personal mission is to create opportunities for growth, development, and success for the people I serve and inform, so it's only fitting that I start with you, my teammates," I say, sticking my chest out in a display of false confidence, wanting him to believe I am the man.

"Wow, I don't believe I've ever heard someone articulate what they're about quite like that. It is a quick, effective way to highlight the difference one intends to make."

"What drives you, Brian? What is it you're about?"

"Well, I haven't thought about this quite as deeply as you have. But what I can tell you is that I applied for this job thinking I was going to teach. That hasn't happened yet. On a personal level, I have a family to support. I also write scripts in my spare time, as you already know. I've completed three so far. It's been my dream to sell one and see it made into a motion picture. That'd be so cool. When that happens, I can say I've made it."

"You don't see yourself teaching for very long?"

"No, not really. Who does? It pays the bills for now. I love teaching, but eventually I'm gonna have to move on."

"You have goals. Something keeps you going—I like that! Let me ask you this before I forget," I say, half lying. "I had an opportunity to chat with Stacey and Shahila separately. They gave me their perspectives on our team' dynamics. What's really going on with them?"

"Everybody wants to do a great job and look good doing it. We work for the same boss and should be doing our share to make the office as a whole look good. People's egos sometimes get wrapped up in the work; they stop sharing and forget we have to play nice in the sandbox."

"That's a very good way to put it, but honestly, you're short on specifics. I'm still a little confused." I start shaking from a belly laugh. "C'mon, talk to me straight."

"I get along with everybody, sir. With all

of these people. They're all very nice to me. Maybe some feel threatened. Brian looks away. I'm not the right person to talk to about this."

"It's okay. I appreciate that you keep your nose clean. That's something I should probably learn to do myself."

"Thanks for lunch, Antoine."

"Anytime, Brian. Let's do this again soon."

I got to keep my word. Brian is looking forward to doing more teaching. I know he will hold me accountable for that promise. He seemed to enjoy hearing me talk; remarked on how having a personal mission statement could be beneficial, and gained insight into my way of thinking; however, I cannot help but feel he resented my bluntness.

Later on, I found out from the boss that although I treaded lightly, the sucker was of a mind that I had practically sought a confrontation with him during lunch. She claimed, he was disturbed that I exhibited no need for validation. I never seem to care what people think of me. Brian disapproves of what he calls my standoffishness. In the few months I've been on the job, I have used words sparingly. Polite, always about business, I spend my days observing people, reading, writing, and listening to the boss.

Now oddly, I feel out of place in this chipper environment, but the boss likes me and wants me to stay. Only God and the devil know why. The team tolerates me. I catch them sometimes looking at me askance. I could swear they're scoffing. One thing is for certain: I'm not messing around!

Within two months, I put a course together. As promised, the opportunity for Brian to teach has finally come. I made it happen. A conscientious fellow, in the classroom his natural inclination is to tell students what he knows, how to behave and what to think. He genuinely wants to help people do better and be better, and acts as if he is the depositor of knowledge, and students, mere receptacles. His lectures feel like PowerPoint-slides-driven sermons. The dude's terrorized at the idea of losing control. His performance must be impeccable. It just has to be! His status, sense of control and identity are wrapped up in it. Yep! I can see he's having a hard time letting go of being the center of attention. We have a problem! He means well, though, but I don't like what I see.

My thing in the classroom is making training engaging and interactive. By making students' thinking visible, bringing out their voices, I find out whether training resonates with them. I give students license to use their best thinking and ideas to shape the training. As a trainer, to allow learning to occur, I must get out of the way and give up some control; encourage students to interact with the material, with each other, and with me. The information I present becomes knowledge only after the students process it through a manipulation of sort.

That sounds loony to Brian. I insist, the real stars in the classroom are always the students, never the teachers. None of the trainers relates to what I am saying, nor do they care to engage in further discussions with me about this. Nothing is happening! I have lost this round. They believe, I too will eventually go away, move on to another position and leave them alone. All staffers do. It's just a game. The pay's not shabby, after all. But I'm on to them. Surviving staffers is only possible if you pretend to care. They're not even pretending.

Not as stubborn as his peers, Brian knows I'm onto something. He notices how students respond to me in class. He wants what he considers the closest thing an instructor can have to power. People come alive with a flutter of anticipation when I get going. I "bring it" every time, he says excitedly. They open up, add insights, and go where I take them mentally. They eagerly discuss the thorniest of issues, and believe in me, he says. And they even try out my suggestions. Brian wants what he thinks I have. People at all levels come to hear the stories I tell and share in the moments I create. It is only conviction and commitment—he calls it "swagger"—and studies what I do in class every time thinking the answers are in the techniques. He's wrong. They can be found in the mindset I bring to the engagement. I've been doing this for twenty-five long years now. If only he knew!

13

Stacey has invited me to a meeting of the managers' advisory team. She's responsible for scheduling it, managing the agenda, drafting and disseminating the minutes. I follow sheepishly. We are climbing down two floors and hurrying through an unending corridor to a conference room big enough for no more than twenty-five people. Teresa is sitting on the sideline where Stacey quickly joins her. The two chat briefly, cozily side by side on stylish Aeron chairs.

Without a view, the room feels oppressive. One wall supports a supersized flat monitor. Sitting atop it, a rotating camera used for videoconferencing focuses on us. A floor-to-ceiling whiteboard for spur-of-the-moment brainstorming sessions serves as an accent wall. Soft dark-gray carpet tiles cover the floor. The faces around the mahogany conference table look familiar. At least ten of them have attended the last off-site in Maryland. This time they look relaxed.

Before the meeting starts, Stacey requests someone explains to those new to the Management Advisory Team (MAT) how the Center operates and the role that the off-site plays in it. A wrinkly engineer starts talking. He's wriggling. There is a glow in his eyes. He seems to love the sound of his own voice.

"What separates us from the rest is our belief in the endless possibilities that technology and the Internet offer intelligence collectors. We've done a good job so far of keeping the country safe. But good is no longer enough. We gotta evolve with the times; otherwise we become irrelevant."

The assembly gasps in agreement.

"We strive to make intelligence gathering smarter and faster. When we're slow, our product no longer qualifies as intelligence—it becomes the news! The antiquated ways of doing the business of intelligence are no longer sustainable. Needs and priorities are constantly shifting. We've not been able to even come close to meeting the needs of our customers lately. There's always more information out there. Our goal's to make it as easy as possible for decision-makers to obtain the intelligence they need. When we focus, we are great, unbeatable. Information no longer resides solely in someone's brain or even in a file cabinet, but on computer systems. We're leveraging multiple access points to that information.

"In more traditional places than our center,

the leadership is made up of a powerful few who make all the decisions about how the work is done and middle managers who enforce these decisions while frontline employees, experts at the work they do, carry out the decisions.

Here, out of necessity, we collaborate and decide together how to get the work done. Leadership and middle managers support, validate and remove bureaucratic barriers to implementation. We turned the pyramid upside down or inverted it, if you will. Does this always work as planned? Well, it depends. Sometimes it does, and sometimes it doesn't, but we keep trying, and we've seen results."

Stacey attempts to get the man's attention. She's been scanning the room.

"Initially the MAT was established to develop a junior-and-midlevel-manager community that would handle strategic and operational initiatives at the Center. This model is being revamped to include officers at every level of the hierarchy, and every grade, to ensure fair representation of the workforce writ large.

"Where does the off-site fit into that model? Well, it serves as a catalyst. It provides a breeding space where ideas can emerge, be debated and fleshed out. Following the off-site, we refine those ideas and brief senior leaders. Everybody is engaged in the process. Brand-new employees as well as seasoned employees, managers, and non-managers participate. We all have a stake in this. In a nutshell that's what makes us different."

What a nutshell! It's so bloated, I wanted to crack it. No one dares ask questions. I'm so happy. The old man said so much, nobody wants to risk causing him to resume his monologue. Not sure I understood everything, but for now his explanation will do!

Although I have other things to do, my desire to please Stacey has caused me to attend the meeting. I'm kicking myself.

14

I now savor my daily sexcapades to Leila's. She keeps me sane. I've become a glutton for her touch. I fancy her more today than I ever did before. She's the closest I have to a best friend. We've started spending more time together. I can be myself with her, funny, intense, silly, or light, anything goes. Our voracious bodies yearn for a taste of each other. There is now symmetry in this newfound passion. I've fallen under her spell, a little whipped, but I don't mind. I'm out of my depth on this one.

Before officially launching the program, I have spent months conceptualizing and designing, I'm convening a meeting with Stacey, Shahila, and Brian. As expected, Lorie wants no part of it and refuses to attend. We meet in a cramped office to discuss the work ahead and divvy up responsibilities. I open by asking colleagues to describe current sources of pride in their lives. Shahila volunteers to share first.

"I love to spend time with my grandson. He's a source of joy. He's smart, adorably handsome and he keeps me young at heart. At work, I recently received more recognition for the work I do with TOC 101. It's so nice to be appreciated."

Brian is nodding. "Good move!"

"Thank you, Shahila. I'm very happy for you. We're on the same team. When you win, we win." I say, trying to placate her.

I choose to overlook the poorly veiled display of scorn coming from Stacey. She's placed herself right across from Shahila. What if I put her on the spot and make her squirm a little?

"What's going well in your life at the moment, Stacey?"

"In my private life or at work?" she asks.

"Whatever you're comfortable sharing."

"Well, I've been providing support to a bunch of important high-level meetings. I prepare the agendas, make sure everyone receives timely updates, keep track of the decisions made, and brief the front office on everything. They've expressed deep appreciation for a job well done. Their words, not mine."

"Super. That's very nice—very nice indeed," I say sheepishly.

"What about you, Brian?"

"After we had that talk, I've been working on improving my platform skills. I can't wait to transition into training full time. Other than that, it's been the same old, same old. Been taking care of the Familiarization courses. Everything's been smooth, but that's nothing new or exciting. Looking forward to what's coming."

"Thank you, Brian. That's why we're here today—to discuss what's next. As you know, the front office wants us to offer a series of courses to train employees in transformational leadership. Rather than start from scratch, I thought it best to build on what we already have that works: things like the Decision-Making course and the Taking Charge course, both taught by Coach David, and the Battlefield courses, the Gettysburg and Antietam courses. Now, I understand that you haven't really provided training in a while, and I intend to give you enough time to prepare and practice before launching. I've developed lesson plans for the new courses and am now ready to share them with you. First, we will offer Transformational Leadership proper, as a two-day flagship course. Then a two-day High-Performance Teams workshop, a Leveraging Difference for Innovation course, a Women in Leadership course, and an introductory two-day Leading like a Coach class, which the four executive coaches will deliver.

"Each of you needs your own area of responsibility. After a while, we may switch those responsibilities around and mix things up a bit. I'll lead the flagship course with you as co-facilitators. Even though we'll each be responsible for different things, we gotta help one another. What d'you want to take on as your primary responsibility?"

"I'd love to work on the High-Performance Teams. The topic appeals to me," says Brian.

"Good. Anyone objects? No? Okay. It's yours, Brian. What about you, Stacey?"

"Anything you say, Antoine."

"Actually, I want you to pick based on what appeals to you, just like Brian did."

"I'm here to do whatever I'm told."

"Okay. I'm telling you to choose. I'd like you to have some ownership. Make your choice. That way, you should be happier and more motivated."

"No, it really doesn't matter."

"I'll give you a little time. What about you, Shahila?"

"Oh, I want the Women in Leadership course. I have a few ideas about how to make it very popular." Shahila is beaming.

"Great. It's yours—unless Stacey wants to fight you for it."

"No, it's all right. She can have it. I'll do

whatever you want me to do, like I said."

"Okay, too sad, too bad. Why don't you stick with the Battlefield Courses, Gettysburg and Antietam, since you've been supporting them anyway? However, as you know, we're losing the adjunct trainer who's currently helping with them. How much time would you need to get up to speed, take the lead, and deliver them yourself?"

"I've been involved with them for five years and have attended every single running. It'll be fairly easy for me to lead them. Been there, done that."

"Great! So, it's settled, then. Now, other than the Women in Leadership course, all the lesson plans have been developed. We'll start offering this particular course in a year. Teresa will tell you more, both about the content and direction that the leadership of the Center wants you to take and about what specific lessons will need to be developed. Those now in charge of the other courses will decide how they want their content delivered and what else they want us to do to support them. Feel free to modify what doesn't work well for you and the students, but whatever you do, before finalizing any plans, share and let all of us know what you're doing so we can weigh in.

"Anyone wants to add anything before we

break? … No? The meeting is adjourned then."

15

I see Devin for the first time on the day of the conference. A pale, lanky, bespectacled fellow with a tuft of straight salt and pepper hair on the skull, he shows up at nine o'clock in the auditorium to welcome everyone. He shakes hands with the senior leaders sitting in the front row, then proceeds slowly to the center of the stage to greet the audience with a gentle circular wave of the hand. Collecting his thoughts, he stands quietly for what seems a full minute before talking. The auditorium is dead quiet.

Distant from the crowd, eyes cast down he nervously clutches a piece of paper above the waist. All eyes are on him. The room is still with expectation. After a few hums to clear his throat, he proceeds to deliver the keynote address. Making eye contact with no one, smiling only faintly, he is causing the audience to strain to hear him. I feel deflated. Unimpressed, after only a moment, no sooner has he said something, I forget most of it, or so I believe. On cue, the room gives a lackluster applause. I am horrified. Is this the man whose vision I'm supposed to help sell? What a letdown! How can I back out of this?

I realize this now, after the fact! My high expectations of Devin have overshadowed the message he's delivered. Words that I found meaningless now resonate in my sleep:

"We must transform this organization if we are to remain relevant to national security. Every one of you must start from wherever you are. If you're not in a formal position of authority, you can still write the memo and take the initiative. You need to lead from where you are, and not wait for approval, permission, or for someone else to take care of the problems. Give yourself permission to do the right thing. If you're a formal leader, you need to shift your focus from command to collaboration, from control to connection, from coercion to co-creation, from a bias toward conformity to a bias toward change, and from the mechanistic to the organic.

The transformation we seek requires a mindset shift from an obsession with answers to a focus on powerful questions, from being comfortable with defined outcomes to becoming comfortable with ambiguity, allowing outcomes to emerge, and from expertise being centralized to expertise being distributed. As leaders, whether formal or informal, if we are to thrive, we need to be in the business of disrupting the status quo. Disruption is the essence of innovation."

16

Leila is becoming restless. She now wishes for permanence. The regularity of our encounters has made them routine. She's comfortable with me around and sees the future clearly. The one she wants.

"Time is of the essence," she says.

"What does that mean?"

"I see two beautiful vanilla babies crying to be born."

A God she does not believe in has assured her of it, in a dream?

In a dream? I'm not having it. Please, come again! What is she talking about? On a whim? This is not how I envision bringing babies into the world.

Seeing my reluctance to entertain the thought, she decides to keep quiet about the dream until the time is ripe again for the telling. I can feel it, she'll be looking for a sign that indicates I'm ready to soften up. I must start using protection.

Shahila, petulant as always, craving recognition, works tirelessly to provide a valuable service and brings more acclaim to the Office of Training. I like her, rude, feisty and all. Yet she enjoys no real support from the rest of the team; surely, because of her grating personality.

Stacey, I know, is mounting an underhanded campaign to assassinate her character and cause her to lose her job. She has enrolled the rest of the team in the personal vendetta. News of the infighting and backbiting spread. The repeated complaints are filtering up. Her superiors will have it no other way; Teresa is forced to address the situation head on.

Stacey has cozied up to many higher-ups, especially the males for whom she performs little unsavory favors. Teresa expects little support from them. Stacey's power lies in the connections she's made over the years.

Teresa is worried. She covets her powerful network. At the next staff meeting, vowing to send a strong signal, she gathers us—Stacey, Brian, Shahila, Lorie, and me—in a tiny conference room. Having been briefed in advance, I know what's going down; how the meeting is about to unfold, and what outcome is expected. I play along, feigning surprise when everyone around the table is asked to pick up a marker to write on the wall. On long decals Teresa categorizes the functions we perform. She then asks us to write our names under the tasks we routinely perform.

The meeting breaks from tradition. Rather than rattling off announcements as usual, this time Teresa is engaging us in an activity. It feels like a game. Everyone takes to it. It gives us a chance to show off what we do. A few teammates even suggest adding a few categories we had all forgotten about.

The exercise over, we take our seats again and wait for further instructions. All doom and gloom, Teresa slowly hands out to each of us a formal description of our jobs. She then instructs us to map the descriptions to our scribbles on the wall and to assess whether or not we are performing as expected the tasks listed in the description. A funny thing happens.

Shock is apparent on my teammates' faces. I shouldn't laugh, so I snicker. The look on their faces tells a powerful story. It turns out, other than me, no one has been doing more than half of what they've been hired to do. Teresa looks relieved. A smug grin betrays her sense of victory. Satisfaction is written all over her mug. As she prepares to dismiss us, she acts as if she's sent a strong message. I cannot take it anymore. I need more clarity, so I open my big mouth.

"Do you all know what this means?"

I look straight ahead, serious, like I'm expecting an answer. Here's Brian to the rescue.

"By the looks of things, unless we step it up, we may lose our jobs," he says.

Teresa fawningly interjects, "Well, that's true, but I trust that you will all do what's necessary to turn things around."

I am livid.

"Here she goes again softening the blow," I exclaim. It's too late to roll it back.

"What did you say?" she repeats.

"All you had to do was let Brian's comment sit awhile and sink in. Sorry, I'm super bad and out of line, I know."

Teresa gives me the stink eye.

I threw her off her game. Nervous and uncomfortable, she speaks again; so much this time. Again, she drowns out the point of the activity. Why does she feel she needs to justify herself? We spend another fifteen minutes cramped in the conference room. The woman is desperate for approval—needing to be liked. She can't help this need to just be the good gal. And we can no longer stand her for it.

The decision had been made. Unless performances as well as team dynamics improved, the contractors would face reductions in pay, and/or job loss. That truth is never spoken that day. All stare blankly, gasping for air. They need a break. I am thoroughly disgusted by Teresa's lack of a backbone. I'm over her.

With the usual avalanche of words, she places pillows around the truth. The message has gotten lost. Servant leader my ass. She is more servant than leader. A gentle person at heart, she suffers from a serious case of self-serving indulgence.

Waffling works for people who are uncomfortable being the boss—for all those who want more than anything to be liked, for those who find silence abhorrent, for those who care more about what others think of them than for what they themselves think of themselves, yes, waffling works.

When Teresa's brain stops working, her mouth goes into overdrive. I can't stand to be managed by a coward. What does that make me? She knows nothing of the freedom that one derives from being true to oneself. She has no capacity to do what is right simply because it is hard, nor the willpower to make decisions based on how she truly feels. All she ever cares about is to keep others happy. I'm not happy and she isn't free.

17

Does she still hold a grudge? Is she still sore about my comment? Two weeks after the incident, I'm still uneasy in the office!

"Water under the bridge," Teresa says loudly as she jerks my arm, signaling I need to tag along to a weekly meeting in her boss' office. Chad is a dapper gentleman, well-liked, gray-haired, medium-built. He has a ready smile and listens with his beady eyes more than he talks. He asks more questions than he makes statements.

To have a real conversation with Teresa is difficult, anyway; one can hardly place a word in edgewise. She literally talks all the time; interrupts constantly, and she hardly listens. Head slightly tilted, eyes open wide, she speaks mostly out of nervousness. We all want to smack her. She is a lady, though.

Either she is avoiding something, or she totally lacks self-awareness, and the social graces that Chad possesses in abundance. I am learning. He is a more patient man than me. Finally, she's coming up for air. With no hint of a smile, Chad looks her straight in the eyes and calmly steals her thunder:

"Teresa, I need that plan I keep asking you

about. I'm done asking. You're late again. Please get it to me as soon as possible. It's been months."

She looks away, opens her mouth to talk.

No, not again. Teresa really needs saving. Some type of intervention. Anything.

Dismissing her justifications with a flick of the wrist, Chad turns to me half smiling and says:

"Please Antoine, rescue Teresa from herself. Help her complete the strategic plan I've been asking her about. Someone told me you were an adjunct in the strategic planning course for managers."

The same day, we got to work on the strategic plan. I have to put up with more bitching and complaining from Teresa. Four weeks later, triumphantly, beaming with pride, she hands the document to Chad. Another box has been checked. The monkey's off her back.

Within the month that follows, the chief of the analytic branch calls on me to help his leadership team finalize its own strategic plan. What's happening here? The branch focuses on five goals. The leadership team identifies three. By interviewing all one hundred analysts, I uncover what they care about most, and end up submitting their two top goals to the leadership team.

The interviews do more than uncover what matters most to the staff. Through crocodile tears, temper tantrums, heartfelt admissions of cowardice, pathological expressions of fear, grandstanding, and bravado, employees reveal dysfunctions in the management that threaten to derail careers and the smooth operation of a key office. Micromanagement, abuses of power, lack of trust, lack of respect, and invalidation add insult to injury and reinforce the nagging sense that management does not have employees' best interest at heart. The perception that only a few are trusted to control every piece of the analytical process as well as the day-to-day routines further contributes to employee-retention problems, low morale, and low productivity.

To let off steam, several teams stay past the hour allocated for our gripe session. Some people follow up with phone calls, e-mails, and personal visits to my office. I convey my findings to the leadership, serve as an advocate for the workforce, and recommend prompt action to turn perceptions around. The chief of the analytic group openly acknowledges the problems brought to his attention, and the staff begins to trust that in all this, I'm an honest broker. Among the managers, I am lauded for succeeding in getting reluctant employees to open up about sensitive issues.

It isn't long before I receive more invitations to help fix teams in crisis. I now frequently meet with disgruntled employees in need of a compassionate ear. My ability to listen, they say, helps them keep things in perspective. They're able to retain a sense of control over their emotions. I assign those I cannot help to the three executive coaches on contract. More work needs to be done, but who's taking care of my needs? How did I end up in this position? It seems dealing with people problems is fast becoming my specialty. I'm the disgruntled one here. Not the other way around. When did I get co-opted? Who did me like that? I work for the plantation, yet the plantation does not work for me.

On four occasions within a two-month period, the Office of Training is abuzz in activity, overwhelmed, really. My job description has expanded. Have I become a square? Currently, I'm obsessing over the mysterious human turds left in plain sight under surveillance cameras; some outside an elevator, some in a stairwell, and yet some, in a hallway — all in one of the most secure buildings on the Plantation. That puzzles me, like everybody else. No one knows exactly who is doing it. Everyone's a suspect. Rumor has it the culprit is a disgruntled manager.

18

It's become a struggle to cozy up to Leila lately. She seems tense all the time and increasingly distant. What happened? No longer nagging for proofs of my affection, she is refusing physical contact now. How bothersome! No therapy for me.

"I'm so sorry. If you need a release, I cannot help you. Not ever again. We need to take things slowly." I sense her rage.

"But…"

She shrugs off my aborted attempt at a response.

"What have I done? Will you not play with me, not even a tantric game?"

She is not amused and does not seem to care. I must have missed something, a sign, or a notice! When did this happen? I almost feel uneasy around her now. She says nothing. I'm oblivious. "Has she been feeling neglected, concerned whether I have changed towards her? Since when is sex an issue between us?"

She withdraws into her shell; is she feeling degraded because of what she calls my single-minded attention to her body? It's a fantasy. Although I cannot say it, I have feelings for her. Maybe she's met someone and no longer fancies me? She's changed. This will not do! I want her to want me. Am I too self-absorbed?

I don't know what to say to her anymore. Leila seems touched, hurt deep down in her psyche. How can I be more kind, considerate, and attentive to her needs? Is it too late? I can still learn to become a more generous man! Now, I feel bad. The world is wrong about me. Nothing revolves around me, I know that. I am woke, am I not?

Has the misbehavior of others given me license to become bad as well? So focused on what was done to me, my drug of choice has become the cause. Let's face it, I'm incapable of loving anyone. I'm just a cruel self-righteous fool enamored with lofty ideals and my own dick. My insecurities and lack of psychological safety have rendered me selfish.

Leila's world has shrunk, there is no lust in it. She's a martyr that endures a freedom she does not want. I have impoverished her, emotionally that is! We feel lonely, disconnected, and free, together. We are slowly motioning towards alienation. Together is a word I need to learn to pronounce correctly.

A small, newly reorganized office in the Center is struggling to retain its staff. Morale is low, productivity, in the dump. The front office wants to overhaul its strategic direction. The executive director believes an off-site could tap the staff's collective intelligence and move the process along. Leveraging a variety of perspectives will be helpful in formulating a robust plan. I'm already at work on a tentative design for the event.

The off-site will take place on a hundred-and-eighty-acre cross-fenced ranch in Virginia's Shenandoah Valley, a beautiful area renowned for its equestrian farms. Adjacent to a national park, surrounded by tall trees, the ranch feels private. Military personnel in civilian clothing posted inconspicuously all around the compound protect the discreet corporate retreat. There is plenty to do here: swimming, trout fishing, hiking, horseback riding, mountain biking, and numerous trails teeming with wildlife. There is also a well-equipped gym.

The Center's front office forces me, the go-to person for all things strategic, upon the chief of the small, newly reorganized office. She stands firm and pushes back as hard as she can. No need for me, she can handle the facilitation on her own, she claims. I am rooting for her because I don't wanna do it; that is, until a zealous secretary comes looking for me to report what she said about me in the meeting. Pushing back against the front office's imposition, I am, she insists, although we've never met, the scum of the earth, a renegade, a person with no breadth or depth.

What have I done to this lunatic?

I show up at the gate after a long drive, to be immediately detained by military police. My name is not on the guest list. I am angry. The chief's passive resistance is vexing. It's become personal. For an excruciating half hour, the arresting officers furiously call to confirm who I am and secure my access to the ranch. An executive from the off-site party is finally dispatched to the gate to clear me.

There is no time for hurt feelings. It's way more constructive for me to consider this hiccup an oversight. Sneaking through the back door into the conference hall, I catch a glimpse of the small-office chief for the first time and tense up right away.

I didn't expect that! What a beauty! The curvaceous bitch worthy of cult-like adoration is floating effortlessly above the crowd. She hovers like a conductor in the middle of an assembly. We've spoken twice; though curt on the phone, her voice had provided no clues of her crushing beauty or utter contempt for me. The symmetry of her distinctive features gives me intense pleasure and, at the same time, blurs my thinking. I am assessing her outside of my conscious awareness, yet I hate her already with a passion.

The chief's scrunched-up face betrays her mounting anger. The resistance from the staff looks fierce, heartfelt, and unyielding. I wake up to the reality of the argument in the room. The chief has the right stuff; she should have been capable of turning the hearts of men. She is adamant, employees should stick to the business at hand, get over whatever has caused them grief in the past. "Today is a new day, and—" All of a sudden, she holds her breath. She's just become aware of my presence; had not wanted me there, yet she sighs in relief. She sure seems glad to see me. I am here honey!

Her nod serves as an invitation for me to take over. Now, I clearly see a smirk on her face, as if she's daring me to do better. She fumbled while trying to focus the attention of the staff and seemed desperate. Now she is neglecting to share her plans with me. Undeterred, I approach swiftly with studied assurance and inquire about the goal for the session.

I fancy me a tall, imposing presence in the middle of the room. Using my booming voice, I introduce myself; request participants explain what they believe their office is uniquely set up to deliver, what it is not delivering, and what the real obstacles are. I make it clear I know nothing and take nothing for granted. The boss has taken the obvious for granted, yet, reality has a way of shifting. I seek to explore the mindsets at the root of their failure.

She'd been attempting to avoid a conflict she cannot manage—but that's exactly what I seek to have more of, a conflict. Managers, I am reminded, favor consensus over conflict which means they compromise the truth, leaving everyone underwhelmed. There is growth in conflict. I'm conflict-confident.

I remind the assembly that conflict arises from people's needs, and needs unmet do not just go away—they lay in wait for the next opportunity to express themselves and get in the way of what matters. It signals that something important is afoot. Our differences generate conflict. Conflict generates change. Without it, attitudes, behaviors, and relationships remain the same. So, let's get into it.

By facilitating conflict, I'm causing options to surface and employees to buy into the process. With the ultimate end goal of producing better decisions. Conflict, I reckon, should improve the quality of their decisions by allowing all points of view, particularly the unusual ones, to be heard. I am using conflict here to hopefully provide the medium through which problems can be aired and tensions released, and I should probably be scared, even a little bit. The enemy is watching from a corner of the room.

Under the chief's miffed stares, I proceed to set expectations for the discussion. There will be no personal attacks. Instead, we will strive for factual specificity and a focus on solutions. I expect facts to support opinions. Conflict around ideas is to be expected, but personal attacks shall not be tolerated. We are all in agreement.

To the chief's dismay, in the hour and a half that follows, the off-site turns into a free-for-all, a cacophony of dissenting opinions, and a gripe session. The chief seems to be enjoying the mess I've made. She is jeering at me. "Are you happy now?" Once the energy fades, I'm pointing out what has been captured on flip charts and confirming that it is all a true reflection of what's significant, indeed the issues these people are experiencing. All agree. The issues they brought up are of no consequence to me. I am not affected by any of them, while they are. They may not have caused the problems either, yet they suffer because of them. These are their problems now, those they're complaining about, not mine, and as such, they must take responsibility for doing something about them. No one else cares, no one else can. Radio silence. Am I getting through? Or, am I getting kicked out?

. An eerie tension engulfs the room. No one argues anymore. The employees have complained enough; they feel plenty understood and are now resigned and ready to roll up their sleeves to get down to brass tacks.

I win! Narrowing the office's priorities then becomes child's play. Passionate and forward-focused conversations ensue. Of the twenty-five goals, they had worked on unsuccessfully last year; they manage to pick the five they believe most crucial to the success of the office.

They work on a strategy that encapsulates the goals. By lunchtime they have agreed on five goals they believe can be reached, and on the rough outline of a winning strategy. They proceed to make a convincing case to the chief arguing why they ought to be allowed to move in the direction they want.

The chief is stunned and pouting at the same time. At that instant, her appeal fades in my mind. The spell is lifted. The whiny little heifer has ceased being attractive! All of a sudden, it's clear how all along her ugly controlling ways were the source of the problems in the office. She wilts before my eyes. A total stranger, one without breadth and depth, has achieved in half a day what she'd been struggling to achieve for months, an agreed upon way forward. In the afternoon and on the next day the offsite participants spend time refining a strategy that is bound to turn their pious vows into operational wins.

19

The feedback he received after the conference alarmed him so much, Devin determined to do better next time. His delivery sucked big time. It almost got in the way of the message. Because of his awkwardness, the change efforts he champions have suffered.

The man's desperately trying to get out of his own way. Determined to polish his presentation skills, once every two weeks now, Devin makes a point of communicating with the workforce in person. In the year that follows, he takes the floor for thirty minutes to an hour every month, at every off-site and at every leadership class we teach.

He resists his natural inclination to withdraw into his shell. His message is finally getting some traction. The efforts are paying off. Within a year, he has transformed before our very eyes; he stands taller, his back is straighter; his smile is brighter; his arm movements are wider, and his demeanor is bold and free. Looking people straight in the eyes now, he emotes, grips their attention, takes up more space, and owns the ground he walks on. At long last, I've become a believer.

Every month, Devin pontificates about the

need for intelligent failures.

"Stop it. If you're not failing, you're not trying hard enough. You're playing it safe, being mediocre. Be bold."

By going deep, doing the hard work of embracing his vulnerabilities, and sharing the lessons he's learned, Devin is coming into his own as a change agent. We can almost hear him roar, loud and clear. The fear's gone!

Rumor has it he's spent so much time with coaches, he's now pursuing certification as a coach. They've worked with him on his executive presence. Within a year, he has clearly morphed into a giant white gorilla making his presence felt. The beta has become an alpha and a total badass.

The Center is getting flooded with requests for employment. The number of outside requests for training has also sharply increased. The empowered rank-and-file are accumulating operational successes and are establishing the Center not only as a serious contender in the intelligence collection game, but also as an employer of choice on the plantation. Devin's influence is growing. People are paying attention to his actions and taking his message to heart.

The energy has become palpable. The foot traffic is maddening. It's electric. There is laughter and noise all around. People are restlessness. Officers play silly games in between bouts of intense concentration. Tempers flare and time evaporates. Amends follow, so does laughter! Intense and prolonged collaboration exposes the dark and the funny side of all.

More often than not, Devin admonishes employees to take more risks. He trusts us, and we trust him. Trust is risk, risk is trust. Trust pays dividends that prompt even more risks, and bigger problems are solved in record times. "Yes, and" is now our new mantra. The culture is getting an upgrade. Devin challenges employees to look for reasons to say 'yes', to life and to possibilities. "Innovation will come from our biggest 'yeses'. It's easy to say 'no'. That requires no effort, and no imagination. The real victory lies in finding ways to say yes more often," he chants.

Many take him up on the challenge. Employee morale is high.

It's official. They identified him as the culprit in the series of incidents that had everyone buzzing. He must have known they were closing in on him. He had it coming. I was leaving the building when the police found the body of an old man around six in the evening.

He'd jumped out of the roof to his death shortly after hearing of his imminent termination. Turd man was the nickname we'd given him. I took a glimpse of his bruised face and gasped. I couldn't believe my eyes. There lied the engineer who had once loved the sound of his own voice at the meeting of the MAT.

20

Leila now imagines the worst whenever I am slow to come visit with her. She won't touch me yet she wonders if I've met someone else. She is so foolish; I can barely stand it. Why is she like that? Just because of my lack of interest in settling down with her? I just can't get myself to make this commitment.

She's turning thirty-two soon. Time is of the essence, that's all she ever thinks about. It makes sense, but I refuse to even consider it. I've stopped asking about why she looks so gloomy lately. The answer might trigger a fight and force me to reconsider our relationship. It is safer that way.

We talk about work and not us. She humors me when she recounts silly office stories about the language school. It's no use venturing to bring up her aspirations for us, convinced as she is I'm not in love with her. I'm downplaying my feelings. On occasions, I show her affection, but there's never the twinkle she expects in my eyes when she's near—only careful calculations and the warmth of a friendship that she no longer tolerates. Although she won't say it, I can feel it, she still wants more. We've learned to coexist in cordial hypocrisy.

I train, mentor, coach officers, and facilitate the transformational change Devin envisioned. Fully on board, I am leading parts of his effort on the training front as best as I can. The people who remember how powerful he made them feel are excited to be part of something bigger, his movement. I'm pushing hard, boldly enticing students to self-actualize. They respect me and take the message to heart. I don't think anyone has ever told them why they should become bigger. I challenge them to find their purpose and a pathway to their engagement; and to make valuable, novel, and surprising contributions. Inspiring leadership in people is my vocation. I have become a minister of the transformational faith.

I too want to become bigger, happier, bolder, and stronger than I've ever been before. That will not happen if I give in to fear. Although I'm still afraid of mice, spiders, and cats, I wish to love myself as if my life depended on it. I need to transform the powerlessness I've internalized. Fear is just a thought whose job is to keep me safe; but in doing so, it also keeps me small and stuck. It is just a thought, all the same! I can kill my self-limiting beliefs by changing my thinking.

A few middle managers have embraced Devin's vision. Not nearly enough of them. The rest are too busy plotting his downfall. Low expectations cause low engagement. They're hanging onto their positions for dear life. Devin is relying on the wrong people to carry out his vision. A diverse bunch, many are quietly resisting. How could they give employees the confidence, autonomy, and resources they need to act on their own best judgment?

What if a lack of common sense led them to fail? What has gotten into me? Feeling sorry for those who shared stories of invalidation with me, I'm approaching groups of managers to make a plea for inclusion. When did I become an advocate? Am I really speaking on behalf of employees here? I find myself explaining how differences generate change; how, whether the change is good or bad depends entirely on managers' capacity to include differences. Inclusion to be real cannot be about forcing differences to conform. They have that all wrong!

With inclusion, employees become eager to express alternate viewpoints; solve problems, acknowledge personal and systemic blind spots; and support for organizational objectives increases, as does trust and effectiveness. Many warmed to the ideas. Others, stared blankly, uncrossed their arms, and wished me good luck.

Providing me top cover, the front office looked kindly to my admonitions, but winced whenever I suggested there is dissension among managerial ranks as a few were sabotaging the work of the director. In their attempts to manage up, middle managers had already elicited sympathies from a top management removed from the day-to-day grind and trusting them more than me.

"Surely," they responded, "you must be exaggerating. Ambition is blinding you." I was clearly overstepping my bounds. Who had made me advisor to the king?

With that big mouth of mine, I never miss an opportunity to dig my own grave. Just because people say they want to know how to leverage diversity and produce innovation doesn't mean they seriously mean that or feel up to it. Who wishes to get comfortable with conflict? I may want leaders to engage with their followers and create a connection that raises the level of motivation and morality in not only the followers but also the leaders themselves; but the truth is, to them, this is all just for show. No one asked me for my opinion and no one cares! I'm a yeoman who must continue to do the grunt work and should shut up already!

21

On a variety of issues, news outlets and Twitter feeds provide more actionable intelligence than we do because, in some cases, they have better access. Devin is seeking to create a stampede that will thwart the loss of relevance and the train wreck that is about to happen.

He continues to communicate his vision every chance he gets.

"If you don't experience resistance, stop what you're doing—nobody cares."

Almost like a chant, he has his message down pat. Every time he speaks, he is rallying foot soldiers to his cause. They come because they believe in him.

"And if you do experience resistance, please, embrace it. Embrace that damn resistance. It means you're doing something that matters. You're ruffling some feathers."

The man is on a mission.

"Only when people free themselves from the constraints of the past can the future be realized. The transformation we want does not create the future by referencing the past. It's not about a better, faster, and cheaper past. That transformation births a future that is entirely new. Yet, it begins with a firm grasp of the current state of affairs and of the past. When you choose the path of transformation, you permit yourself to envision the future freely. There is no clear destination. There is uncertainty, unpredictability and even chaos.

We are creating something that has never existed, and that requires a change in mindset. We need to be the first to transform. Let us create a vision for transformation and a system that continually questions and challenges our beliefs and assumptions. The realization that everything needs to change so we can ensure the survival of the organization is at the root of our desire for transformational change. The current thinking here is limiting, flawed, and incomplete. Most organizations do not think. They react."

I never tire of hearing such idealism. I wholeheartedly want Devin to be succeed.

He did it! Unbelievable! He did it! By ten that September morning, two thousand people had clicked the link Devin had posted at nine thirty. They've watched the twenty-minute video he made. It has interrupted the status quo and brought the place to a standstill; it has jolted everybody into a state of frenzy, and unmistakable awareness. Devin has washed the organization's dirty laundry in public; divulged the tenor of hushed conversations and forced the willfully blind to see what they would not see.

Raising inconvenient truths through questions that trigger thought, the video has started a shit storm. All hell is about to break loose! For decades, we followed the same script without a second thought, built widgets, served customers, run spies, produced analyses, and conducted business as usual. The well-oiled machine produced what it has always produced: more of the same, the status quo. Fear, apathy, and self-doubt kept fueling the disengagement of the many. A stovepipe mentality, a single focus on self-preservation and mindless conformity have caused even more problems, the least of which is groupthink! Yet while we remain the same, the world outside is undergoing unprecedented change.

The video provides no relief from the truth. The images crowd out denial and doubt. They disturb a fragile peace and unsettle the soul through the questions they raise:

"Is the way we've always done things good enough? Is our culture preventing us from changing? Is the status quo adequate, acceptable, and tolerable? Are we doing everything possible to stay ahead of the threats? Are we as bold as we imagine we are? Are we working harder but not smarter? Are we doing what we can rather than what we must? Are we still relevant? Feeling vital? Do we have a September tenth level of satisfaction?"

Many find the questions discouraging. Most are proud to bear witness to the transformational change under way. In it, they share a common identity. By reassessing old ways of thinking, they are becoming part of the solution and beginning to see themselves as stakeholders, more than mere employees. They aspire to less rigidity, more fluidity, an environment that facilitates work at the cutting edge of daring and innovation; one that is free of bureaucratic bottlenecks. They are dreaming bigger, bolder dreams.

Something is going on with me. I can feel a change happening inside. I'm becoming an "intrapreneur." Witnessing what's happening, I feel an intensely pleasurable, almost orgasmic sensation.

With a twenty-minute video, Devin has articulated a sense of urgency for change. Within the hour, someone leaks it outside of the Center, all the way to the seventh floor of the main Plantation building. An hour and thirty minutes after its release, the top dogs have banned the video. It is removed from the network. With the finality of a sentence, an announcement comes down like a judge's gavel:

"Devin is retiring effective immediately." The truth cost him his job. How else can I think of that? The man put his concern for the mission before his job security. Or maybe, it isn't so! Maybe he knew he had nothing to lose, and therefore could afford to push for the change he thought necessary. In any case, he had dared to courageously dance to the tune of a different drummer. Maybe he was simply trying to satisfy his need for self-aggrandizement. That I will never know. And I don't care. It's never been about Devin, really. Change is never entirely about the leader, anyhow. It's always about us!

In the weeks that followed, more people requested to see the infamous video. Expecting the worse, some of us had quickly downloaded it and made copies. Entire offices are organizing viewings, facilitating discussions in order to process what has happened. Its message is taking on a life of its own. Outsiders are showing a keen, unrelenting interest. Banning it made it virtual. Devin's superiors demonstrated their dislike for any change they did not control. *As if…*

22

Being allergic and a little scared too, I hate the scraggly alley cat outside my window. It sleeps in the opening of a storm drain on the lawn that connects three adjacent apartment buildings. A few Buddhists in the neighborhood make weekly food offerings to the unsightly beast in direct violation of the condo bylaws. The biggest transgressor is not a Buddhist however, but a middle-aged Christian woman whose bay window has a direct view of the storm-drain opening.

The cat lady, not content to care for four magnificent purebred felines that never leave her apartment, is hell-bent on rescuing the alley beast. Early in the morning and early in the evening, she leaves plastic bowls outside for an animal that runs from her every time, refusing to be petted. Shaggy, it is choosing to forgo the comfort of human touch to follow its natural instincts. I like that. Though she'd never bring the feral beast inside, the woman seems to love the cautious cat—obviously, a love not reciprocated, and she keeps feeding it. I tried to feed it once, making sure it could see me trying. The damn animal spurned my effort by allowing my milk to turn.

The cat failed to show up by the neighbor's bowl one morning. Oddly enough, I panicked. What prompted me to care? Go figure! Over the course of three years, that cat, ugly as it is, has grown on me. It commands my respect. Come hell or high water, through blizzards, rain, and snow, the tough little rascal survives. Icy conditions, mean kids, and sweltering heat are no match. Through it all, it's proven resilient. For me, it serves as a symbol of what I must become. I like a cat that trusts no one—a smart, resolutely independent, miniature version of a tiger. I love tigers; they're my favorite animal. The day it disappeared, I realized how much it meant to me. Overcome with sadness, I considered the choices before me. Rugged independence or blissful servitude. The revolution is over. What's next? Is there anything else?

The excitement gone and the mood somber, the Center has become a shell. People are busy taking down all evidence of a transformational revolution. Boredom is back. Without a second thought, employees have resumed building widgets, serving customers, running assets, producing papers, and conducting business the way it's always been done. The machine is cranking up to produce what it's always produced, more of the same fear, apathy, disengagement, doubt, silos, focus on self-preservation, and people problems. Once again, life at the Center has become ordinary. My morale is in the toilet where I spend too much time. I would do well to get over myself and flush, but I can't. Truth is, something in me has come alive. I'm unfit for the old new order. Even for a dollar, I don't wanna feel dead ever again.

A creative bureaucracy? What were we thinking? The words seem to cancel each other out. From an intrapreneur to a mere employee, the trip back seems painful and feels forced. *Ouch!* We're clocking in and out and going through the motions again. A few mourners are saying they saw Devin full of promise exit the building on his way into a scary, wide-open world, never to be seen again. They say, his spine was straight, he held his head high; his chin, level; and his chest, relaxed. He was harboring a confident smile and had a twinkle in his eyes before riding in the sunset. It is time for me to go. I too have stopped being afraid of freedom.

23

Leila despairs of ever possessing me. I have changed before her very eyes into a willful, uncontrollable, egomaniacal, yet self-possessed bundle of convictions. I have lost all levity. I have become too intense, too intransigent, and too full of certainties. She feels inadequate, bashful, unworthy even, in my company. Other than shit my pants, nothing I do gets a laugh out of her any more. Yes, she can offer me nothing I care to have anymore.

From a playmate, she's become a promise of indentured servitude. I am not suited for this lifestyle. Never have been and never will be! I am simply not shooting for normalcy. She has grown complacent. I will not blame her. The sacrifices her grandparents made have helped make her life cushy. Is this not what we all want? Yes, and I do too, but not like that. On my own terms.

She senses that we've already lost each other. She had longed for the comfort of the predictable—a life of domestic bliss, tranquility and security. I do not want to know what that is. I was shaped by struggle, for struggle. I am a volcano and a tornado, all in one. She dreamed of living in some faraway tropical place, maybe my island, on a farm filled with the fuss and laughter of two adorable kids and many animals, wrapped in the love she deserves.

She satisfices, and thus, could never follow me into a rough life of courage, discomfort, and wishful thinking. It is too hard for the soul. Mine is already broken. I am scooping the pieces. She was not built for that. Why would I blame her? I did not choose that life. It has chosen me though I have tried my best to let it go. She believes in nothing in particular, and in everything in general. She is naïve. Being a good person is something we both can agree on, but even then, our definitions do not match. She does not like her job, but it pays the bills. Predictability matters! The void my lack of love leaves in her life has to be filled. She does not have to work, but she does it anyway.

In her eyes, my appetite for freedom is rabid; no amount of material success can ever satiate me. This is not what I am after. She does not understand me. This is what everybody wants, she says gently. Instead, I measure success in terms of my experience of joy. The way I feel. I am an addict. Only a cause greater than I, can satisfy my soul. She wonders why I cannot be like other men—satisfied with watching, playing, and discussing sports;

racing cars; making money; and making babies. Short of pulling off her panties, nothing she does excites me anymore, and that barely does it. I am ashamed. Have I become soulless? We have nothing to talk about anymore. Just small talk and I am not good at that. Therefore, we stopped talking. I walked out the door one day without saying goodbye, never to be seen again. Two years after the breakup, I found out she had found her soulmate, was with child, and had married again. I smiled. I am happy for her!

Two weeks after Devin's forced retirement, drowsy from a restless night, I arrive to work early. As soon as I appear on the system, Teresa summons me to her office via instant messaging. The note is terse. I rack my brains trying to recall what I may have done wrong. I dislike summons to the boss's office. Who does not? Expecting the worst, I begrudgingly leave my comfortable chair and make my way to Teresa thirty feet away. I hesitantly knock on the frosted glass door, concerned that I might have violated some secret rule of office politics, wondering whose feelings I might have hurt this time.

Teresa's eyes are sunken and red. Her face is lowered. She looks distressed. The smeared mascara screams. She's been crying. Ready for a tongue-lashing, I pull up a chair to get close to her, as I've done many times. She just wants to talk. Phew. I'm relieved! The moment calls for lending a supportive ear. The desk covered in files piled high above her chest makes her look overwhelmed and small.

"Please, close the door behind you," she says faintly. Teresa is stern. She needs to vent. Because she can count on my discretion, she's become way too comfortable venting to me. I am, after all, her most loyal employee.

Nervously dabbing her eyes, she launches into an account of the events that are causing her grief.

"The staff are not taking me seriously. A year ago, I'd asked you all to develop lesson plans for a groundbreaking class 'Women in Leadership'. There's great demand for classes like this here. It's scheduled to start next January. We're running out of time."

"Yes, a few people have to do some more work. Brian and I have made this request a priority and completed our lesson plans within weeks of you asking."

"Yes, but a year later, Stacey, Shahila, and Lorie still haven't done theirs. A couple of days ago, this late in November, Stacey sent me an email in which she states she was just beginning researching her lesson and wanted to interview a retired officer who'd published a book on the subject. Can you believe this? Lorie offered to help. She'd contact the author whom she knows personally. Are you shitting me? The interview will end up costing the office a boatload of money. "Would that be okay?" she asked. Antoine, can you believe the gall of that woman?

At the end of the email, Stacey recommends hiring the damn author to teach instead of her, and why not, she said, she wrote a book on the topic? After all, she knows the content better than anyone does. A brilliant idea, for sure! The nerve of that woman!"

I'm loving the way Teresa mimics Stacey feigning outrage, and am repressing the urge to burst out laughing.

"In my reply I focused on the need to quickly finalize the lessons. I stressed we had to be clear and compelling and then asked, 'Have you read the material and the book itself? For these lessons we don't need every detail...You need to get students to think, discuss the material, and answer questions. So, what questions do you still have?'"

She must need my validation. Teresa gives me a smug self-congratulatory look. I let out a sigh of relief and am now smiling broadly. She's finally done venting.

Early on, months ago, she'd brushed me off when I suggested to her that a few of our colleagues had no idea how to write a lesson plan. Stacey had not only failed to design a lesson; she also had not read any of the books. Others had pointed that out, as well, to no avail. Always the better angel, Teresa gave everybody the benefit of the doubt. Now, she is livid, kicking herself.

Whenever you ask her to do something, Stacey's initial reaction is to look for someone else to cover for her. Unlike Lorie, she never turns down a request or a tasking, she simply never completes it herself. I reckon, it may be because she doesn't know how to do what she's handsomely paid to do. Lacking confidence in her abilities, she avoids losing face by admitting she feels incompetent.

Budgetary constraints require an efficient use of resources. The boss had tried to warn us. Contractor's pay must align with job functions. Some on the team are not pulling their weight. Lorie has rejected an essential part of her senior-trainer position—instruction—and elected to perform petty administrative tasks instead. Several months ago, Teresa's superior had asked inconvenient questions. She targeted Lorie first, the fat ass sitting duck, and docked her pay by $30,000. Take it or leave it. The choice was clear. No one felt bad for her. she had it coming! The writing had literally been on the wall. Drastic additional actions were warranted, and yet Teresa, dreading a showdown to the point of losing sleep, was terrified of facing Stacey next.

It's about time, I thought on my way out of Teresa's office. I sauntered back to my desk, put out some feelers to gauge the tension in the air, and sat down to scan my computer for Teresa's reply to Stacey… Indeed, I was copied on it. I read the note before settling down to work. I had a lot on my plate.

24

Ten minutes later, an angry conversation interrupts my concentration. Stacey's chair is four feet away from mine. Lorie is griping about Teresa's reply to Stacey's note ten feet away across an aisle leading to a printer. Stacey must have forwarded it to her.

"Why is she asking all those stupid questions? Is she pretending not to get it? Your request is clear. She mustn't want us to do it. As if all we care about is that stupid class. It's so unreasonable if she expects you to produce a lesson like that. She's so fake! Like this man over there, they must want you to fail."

No, she didn't! What? I can't believe my ears. Is she talking about me? Fake, who, me? I feel trapped and triggered. Tired and aggravated, I'm intent on ignoring Lorie, trying as hard as I can to ignore the outburst, but I can't. It's too late. Lorie's hijacked my attention. I've been baited into a fight.

We share an open workspace that offers no privacy. All of a sudden, I'm torn, wishing to right the wrongs. I feel this urge to prove my attackers wrong; aching to defend myself and the boss from slanderous accusations. How did this happen? When did the lines get blurred? I probably identify too much with the boss. Something's happened to me. Do I have a crush on Teresa? When she's needed me, I've been there for her! I've helped turn her goals into reality and have been the strongest performer on her team. How did I come to find myself going above and beyond in my support of management's agenda? I am just an employee. Compliance is all that's ever been required of me. When did I fall for this 'we are a family' bullshit? What happened to boundaries?

Why am I getting consumed with the rantings of a raving lunatic? Why do I even care?

All I ever really have to do is stay black and keep out of people's beeswax. When did I lose myself? This affection for a boss who supposedly has my back is misplaced. Utterly! This is not my fight. I'm not a manager.

It's not the first time Lorie disparages the boss and the work of the team. She makes it abundantly clear she doesn't care who hears how she feels. Now, she's trying to provoke me, again. Had the bosses done what they're supposed to do, we wouldn't be here.

Taking deep breaths, I start in a calm voice, address Stacey and ignore Lorie. I can't stand that lazy bum. Maybe, Stacey will see the light. She's more reasonable than Lorie.

"The boss has your best interest at heart, and just like me, she wants you to succeed. It's in nobody's interest to have a team that flounders. If anything, she wants to help, and wishes you'd ask for the right kind of help."

"But that's what I've been doing, Antoine."

"I know you believe that, Stacey. You gotta be mindful of the impression you give, though."

"What do you mean?"

Even though the conversation is even-keeled, I am treading on dangerous ground and not realizing it.

"Every time you're asked to teach a class, you find some unsuspecting sod to teach it for you. They have their own work to do, and you burden them with yours. How do you think the boss feels when their managers call to complain? Their people are being pulled away from important work."

"I didn't know that. Believe me! They say yes, so I assume it's no trouble at all."

"I hear you! Aren't you afraid some people may start asking questions like why you're getting paid to do a job you never do? Why we even need you here?"

Lorie's loud voice interrupts the conversation. All of a sudden, I feel triggered again. The hairs on my neck stand up.

"Uh, little boss man, you expect her to do

what again? Read all that crap and teach it, too? Are you crazy?"

Ignoring her comment, intent on addressing Stacey, I continue:

"We're all expected to perform the job we were hired to do, Stacey."

Relentless, Lorie is on the offensive again. "It's too much. You hear me? You guys should do this crap yourselves. Leave her alone."

My patience's been sorely tested. I haven't had enough sleep. I'm hungry, and in no mood for this, right now. I do not believe Lorie cares particularly about Stacey's predicament. It's a pretext for her to vent how upset she is about the money she lost. Everything is a slight. She won't get off her ass and go find another job, but instead lashes out at whomever is closer to management. I'm game. Lashing out at the boss will cost her the job. Lashing out at me... Uh... different story. Am I supposed to bear the brunt of her anger and not retaliate? Am I a dummy?

Emotionally hijacked, reeling from the verbal assault of a sloth; disgusted by the cowardice of a conflict-averse manager, I let out a loud and well-deserved snub.

"Fatso, you don't wanna be a trainer, right? Why don't you mind your own damn business, right now?"

The words barely passed my lips, I knew there would be hell to pay. Where did the desire to get involved in office intrigues come from? Am I on a power trip? Was my active mind scanning the office for shit to get into today? Am I desperate for recognition? What monster was I trying to feed? Looking down on Stacey and Lorie, and feeling self-righteous, I probably somehow got the notion I could fix them. If only they would listen, right? Wrong! By claiming I want to help people, am I jockeying for power and authority? What the hell is wrong with stupid, stupid, me?

An outburst, a wingding! That will do! I just handed Lorie the alibi she needs to exact her sweet revenge. I've raised my voice at her using demeaning language. Oh lord. That is huge and unforgivable. Now she will have me nailed to the cross for creating a hostile work environment. Oh, bother!

In the days that follow, otherwise apathetic teammates immerse themselves in a flurry of activities with the sole purpose of getting me fired. They notify the front office. Everyone within earshot has to know what kind of awful person I truly am. I am the big jerk who's traumatized an entire office of angels. Some claim, I pointed a menacing finger in Lorie's face. Others, that I slapped her silly. Still others claim, I spit in her face. A few decent people from HR simply state the facts: I have raised my voice in frustration, called Lorie 'fatso', remained in my seat, and maintained some distance from her the whole time.

The mood has shifted in the Center. Those who've been associated with Devin's Cultural Revolution are moving on and switching jobs. The people who remain have no stomach for change. In the face of slanderous accusations, hoping for fairness would be a stretch. I am one of the last crazies—and the weakest link at that. I hold no title; have no formal authority; enjoy no cover now; and, to top it all off, I look as guilty as sin. I curse, I'm big, I'm bald, and to boot, I'm dark as hell. Oh boy. That's just a perfect recipe for getting fucked. All manner of fanciful accusations will stick. The front office is turning its back on me in much the same way it is erasing Devin's legacy. Teresa is making feeble attempts to exonerate me, and for a full week, acrimony prevails.

25

The big boss is considering the situation dispassionately, and placating the complainers. At the end of the week, he will be announcing his verdict. I receive a formal reprimand. He allows me to keep my job. My accusers, on the other hand, have to go.

The same day, security escorts Stacey, Lorie, and Shahila out of the building. Brian continues in the office for another two years before moving on to a different assignment.

In private, the big boss thanks me for having the fortitude to own up to what I did and for reporting the incident immediately. He knows the training staff has been unsupportive, and that they've done the absolute minimum they could get away with.

"They've stretched the truth enough to make you unrecognizable. Not to worry! I've been following you. I think I understand the type of person you are. We all do. With you, what we see is what we get."

Chad cautions me against appearing too focused on the bottom line at the expense of the people.

"Neglecting politics, much like neglecting the feelings of others, can derail a career.

Remain mindful of your social surrounding, and please, learn from this experience. Take the lessons to heart. Keep a cool head, and don't let people see you sweat again. At the end of the day, none of this is life or death. But understand, if there is a next time, you may not get a second chance!"

I appreciate Chad's benevolence. No one has ever schooled me like this before. Work is war.

"When we push the system, it pushes back. When we push people, they push back. With change comes a lot of resentment. Someone is bound to lose something they hold dear. To those who favor it, the status quo offers a sense of identity and control. The stronger you become, the more people tend to feel threatened and insecure. And naturally, they plot your demise."

I later learned from a secretary that the decision to let go of Lorie, Shahila, and Stacey had been made months before the incident. The blowup was a pretext, the perfect coverup. It offered the chief of training an excuse to assuage her conscience. In the devious scheme of things, I was simply the fall guy. In spy fashion, a staple of the leadership style on the Plantation, duplicity prevails.

Many obscure the truth of their cowardice

behind a devotion to God. The problems are documented—the biggest of which, risk aversion, and an inability to take decisive action coupled with lack of accountability. Everyone pontificates, yet standing between problems and solutions there is a lack of vision and backbone, what we call a bureaucracy, often made up of spineless people with big titles and little influence. Their leadership is a timid, fearful, and ineffectual sham. Too busy looking good and covering their butts, these leaders are more concerned with their next promotion. Bureaucracies are like cemeteries—they are places where ideals go to get buried.

What kind of Plantation are they leaving behind? A wealth of transactional managers and a paucity of transformational leaders make for a bleak future. I want no part of it. Stuck in a game of catch-up, foot-dragging and egomania, they are shaping a corporate culture of narcissism, self-congratulation and mediocrity. The enemy is already here, it is inside; it is fear; it is in us, it is us. Processes designed to mask fear abound. Ego-coddling, tiptoeing around insecurities, and catering to the whims of the anointed, I want no part of this. Go along with the program. Win. Get your next promotion, you hear, and keep your pretty little mouth shut. I want no part of that.

"Smokes and mirrors. I am all about the mission." Shut up! The mission, what is that? You killed it; means nothing anymore. No one cares. Really! Just show me the money! I don't want your treadmill.

Just another code word. Just another hustle, another pretext to cover your greed. The defenders of freedom are afraid of the freedom they defend. Take cover. Protect your ass, your shit's in it.

Take them back, I do not need your illusions anymore. Can't you see, I am stepping toward a stronger identity. I am transformed. You can like me or love me. It's up to you. I no longer give a damn. No matter which direction the wind blows, I live, until I live no more. It has never been about the wind! My brain needs a victory too!

Seeking to create a life of significance for myself, I am finally leaving the Plantation. It's been good knowing you! Almost there, almost free, inching closer to joy, still on a journey to self-actualize. I have finally transformed the powerlessness I internalized into forward movement. Can you dig it? Can you see me stepping out of my comfort zone? I am fly, baby. The hero in my own comic book, not that square, afraid to dream, to live and die with his own shadow. I now own my valleys and my peaks, my demons, and the better angels of my nature. I'm finally moving to the places that scare me. Yes, I am superfly.

I am proud. So very proud I could burst. Fear is just a thought I do not nurture anymore. It has vacated the premise of my soul to make room for audacity. I am offering myself to the wide-open World, now. What we need, right? What we need most is to finally own our voice, live our values, and keep faith alive. Fierce, fearless, and almost whole, I have become my faith, my breath, a Maroon, untamed, in the concrete jungle, independent and willing to live on my terms, not yours. Choosing freedom over brain death.

I want to be dead to you, Babylon!

Free at last, free at last. Thank God almighty, I'm free at last.

By the same author

Christophe, Michel. Chronique d'un Noir à la dérive. ProficiencyPlus, 2016.

—. Deux semaines en janvier. ProficiencyPlus, 2016.

—. J'aurais été un Dieu. ProficiencyPlus, 2017.

—. Le Conservatisme Noir Américain. ProficiencyPlus, 2016.

—. Teaching for Transformation: Teaching from the Heart. ProficiencyPlus, 2016.

—. Broken Happy. ProficiencyPlus, 2017.

—. The Harder the Pain: A Compilation. ProficiencyPlus, 2017.

—. Au Royaume de mon Père. ProficiencyPlus, 2018.

—. Miette d'Empire ou la Tentation du Déni. ProficiencyPlus, 2021.

https://michelnchristophe.com/